# THE SUNLIGHT LIES BEYOND

# THE SUNLIGHT LIES BEYOND

## A NOVEL BY

## JUSTIN KURIAN

REGENT PRESS
BERKELEY, CALIFORNIA

# THE SUNLIGHT LIES BEYOND

# Chapter 1

Although located in the old city center and connecting two major city squares, Iuliu Maniu was an extraordinarily quiet street. It seemed isolated from the rest of the center, and on bright days the sunlight reached its narrow surface for only one or two hours. Few reasons existed to pass through it, as two wider streets lined with businesses ran parallel on either side. Iuliu Maniu had no stores or bars or restaurants, only centuries-old apartments and an abandoned building. John Arden knew this would not last; retail would one day discover the street and take over, but he relished in its serenity while knowing the population rambled about just several hundred feet away.

He climbed the worn limestone stairs to his apartment on the top floor, the third floor, of a building in the center of Iuliu Maniu. His heavy keys, elongated and iron, were the type John imagined one would use to enter chambers in a medieval monastery, and he was fascinated each time he employed them. He had not believed such keys still existed. They were not efficient; he needed to jostle them in the lock for several seconds before they aligned, but when they finally caught, they rewarded him for his travails with a sharp clack as the lock opened.

He poured the wine immediately. At all times he kept a minimum of seven bottles of red in his pantry, since, of course, one must always be prepared for exigencies. Wine in Romania was inexpensive at this time; the hardest part was toting the cases through the city streets and up to his apartment. He gulped the purple, bitter fluid and refilled his glass He then snapped on the lights, as it was already dark outside.

In the living room he was greeted by the substantial chill present in all six of the mostly unfurnished rooms of the apartment. The walls were stone and the ceilings were high, and though it had been a warm October day, the building failed to absorb the heat. So he lit the tall soba knowing at least an hour would pass before warmth began to emanate from its maroon ceramic tiles.

Not surprisingly, Cosmin wanted to visit. He had left three phone messages stating his desire to meet around seven. John had not responded to any of these, but this would not serve as a deterrent. Soon a knock would resound from the heavy front door. If, or more precisely, when, he ignored it, Cosmin would simply knock progressively harder until John responded out of concern for neighbors, whom, of course, he had not bothered to meet.

When John actually did open the door nine minutes later, Cosmin's eyes flickered and he grinned widely, his signature reaction upon seeing John. A leather satchel hung from his shoulder and he raised a bottle of red wine in a pitiable attempt to gain access through the blocked doorway. It worked; John received the offering and Cosmin darted into the apartment, grin intact.

Cosmin was already seated in the living room when John entered with two glasses. He poured the wine and sat back and nodded arbitrarily at Cosmin's comments. Cosmin lauded another suspect bar located in some immemorial cavern and recommended they arrive early. John would protest, but after a few more glasses he would vaguely accede, debasing a delighted Cosmin in the process, and they would depart.

"This is not a bad wine," Cosmin said, touching the top of his shaved head.

"No it's not. It is an awful wine."

"Let's not exaggerate, it's OK," Cosmin pleaded.

"I might attach more weight to your assessment if I had ever heard you say otherwise concerning any of the poisons we have imbibed,"

"And yet you drink it, and accept foulness?"

"I allowed you in here, did I not?"

Cosmin spit wine back in laughter as he patted John on the shoulder and refilled their glasses.

"Taverna," Cosmin said. He grabbed his glass and sipped. "I have heard Taverna is supposed to have good drinks at low prices, and it's always full. It's over in Grigorescu, so taxi."

A lone bulb hung from the ceiling. The harsh brightness concentrated in a tight circle around the bulb, and the rest of the ceiling was darkness. He had not bothered to refasten the translucent glass covering since he had replaced it three weeks ago. It rested, covered by a thin layer of dust, on the floor beside him.

Cosmin left for the pantry. John closed his eyes and felt the softness of the immense cushioned chair on the back of his head and breathed the faint mildew odor. It must have once been an elegant piece of furniture. He reached and stroked the leather cover of a book atop one of the stacks he harbored in his apartment; books of varying types and genres that he had collected in the last months and spent hours a day reading. They were amassed in teetering piles alongside his bed and in the living room. A cork popped and he opened his eyes.

"These damn plastic corks," Cosmin said, tossing the beige knob onto the table before them. "It's not the real Portuguese cork.

That's what keeps a wine proper." He refilled their glasses.

"I don't believe a single wine bottle has ever survived here for more than a day, so let us not overly concern ourselves with its 'keeping'."

Cosmin smiled, rubbing the dark stubble on his cheeks. "So Taverna. Supposed to be always full."

The wine was bitter but John rolled it in his mouth, the acridness clinging to his palate while Cosmin theorized about why Taverna was so successful and why an immediate departure was requisite. John checked the bulb again and tried to convince himself that tomorrow he would fasten the glass covering; it would spread the light evenly.

Two hours later they headed towards the center piata to hail a taxi. In Cluj, in the city center, taxis were commonplace. For a driver's neck to constrict upon hearing John recite an address was not exceptional, for the driver assumed that John was foreign, perhaps American, and had money and might tip well. Few foreigners were in Cluj. Yet the drivers also inferred, from his tone, that he was not new to the city, so distending the fare by driving in circles was not an option.

"Taverna. Grigorescu. On Strada Napoca," Cosmin said. The car jerked forward. Many of the streets in the city center were narrow and laden with potholes, and they jostled about the back seat. Cosmin's enlivened voice was expatiating on American politics and foreign policy and how he possessed an objective perspective on these subjects since he was a Romanian, and he emphasized just how much more he knew than his graduate professors. John listened to segments, or, to be more precise, portions of segments.

It began to rain, pattering an irregular cadence upon the car's rusted roof. John watched the water collecting on the windows and the drops journeying down glass. The streets were poorly lit but when they passed a light the drops would momentarily glow. He pressed his fingertips to the pane hoping to feel the drops in their moment of warmth. The taxi crossed a tiny bridge over the Somes River, and they drove parallel the Parcul Central. The buildings were no longer of the lovely ornate and crumbling stone architecture comprising the old city center, but had transformed into the concrete block structures hastily erected by the communist regime after the Second World War and prevalent in the outer areas of Cluj.

The driver rolled down his dripping window, liberally contributing to moisture levels by expectorating into the rain, and searching until he found somewhere proximate to the address. As he drove away, John listened to the sound of the taxi's tires skidding on water and he looked up at an apartment building's black windows. The buildings on this particular street were still turn of the century domiciles. Little could be seen: the streetlamp at the end of the block provided the sole illumination, and lacked munificence with its offering. Thumping noise from bass music escaped from somewhere below, but no visible signs of a bar were evident. This was not uncommon in Cluj; one had to possess the address or the bar did not exist. Chilly rain unremittingly fell but John did not notice his clothes dampening. Cosmin ventured down a barely visible staircase, returning quickly and breathing rapidly as he informed John that this was indeed the Taverna.

The music increased tenfold with the opening of the door. Another flight of stairs awaited in the darkness. As John climbed down, watching his feet contact each stair, he breathed the moist air heavy with the pong of rotten alcohol. A dim bar crouched in the far end of the room. The stone arches lining the ceiling were scarcely discernible, but it was apparent this tomb was here long before the building above. Round tables, filled with drinkers, were obstacles on the sodden floor as they ventured toward the bar. What light existed escaped from low wattage bulbs swaying from the ceiling.

"Two vodkas," John told the bartender. The first gulp burned his tongue, but this was mollified with a second. The spirits behind the bar were predominantly vodkas from Romania or Hungary, and the few bottles from Italy or Spain were unopened. And numerous bottles, label free of course, were filled with local palincas, and lurked on the lowest shelf and beneath the bar.

"Do you want to sit?" Cosmin asked, waiting for John's approval.

They sat in silence at a nearby table. "This isn't a bad bar," Cosmin said, his eyes focused intensively on John.

"Oh?"

Cosmin swallowed vodka. "Not so bad," he said, still monitoring John. Fits of fierce coughing escaped from a tenebrous corner.

"Yes," John said, "your taste is sublime."

Cosmin erupted in laughter.

"Another drink?" John asked.

At the bar John ordered more of the same. He avoided resting his elbows on the thick plank, as its surface was murky liquid.

"Do you like it here?"

John turned and a slender woman was beside him. Her dark hair and piercing features were barely discernable, as they melted into the dimness. The bartender filled the glasses.

"I don't know."

"What does that mean?" she asked, smiling. "One either likes a place or not. There is no middle."

John raised his drinks off the bar, and their damp bases wept into the putrid puddles beneath. "Perhaps, but I made no reference to a middle. I said I don't know." He returned to the table and a grateful Cosmin.

"What was she asking?" he said, eagerly. "What did she say?"

"Very little."

"To hell with you. An attractive woman says hello at a bar and you ignore her." John didn't respond. "You're fortunate and ridiculous," Cosmin continued. "With your looks that happens all the time. Now me, what do I get? My last girlfriend throws me out and I can't find anything since." With three strokes of his lighter, each increasingly spasmodic, he lit his cigarette and went searching for a bathroom.

John smelled his vodka and thought of bandages. Something crunched under his foot, but he refrained from checking the sound's origin. The chair beside him shuddered, and the woman from the bar sat down.

"Do you mind?" she asked, staring at John. "I'm actually not fond of this place."

"You are forced to come here?"

She paused. "I'm just making conversation."

"All right."

"You are from America?"

"Does it matter?"

"I'm curious."

"Yes." Another object crunched beneath his foot.

"What are you doing here?"

John's vodka vanished with a full tilt of his glass. He did not see Cosmin.

"Well?" she asked.

"I'm savoring the atmosphere."

After a silent pause, she exploded into raucous laughter. "No, why did you ever leave there?"

John positioned his glass vertically, hoping to reap a few itinerant droplets, but all was barren. He stood and walked through the dimness. He found the stairs. He did not look back. Outside the raindrops whipped randomly in the wind. By the end of the street he was heavy with water and he wiped his eyes with the back of his right hand. The water tasted briny. Two poorly lit streets were before him. A can clattered against the pavement. He did not know if the street to his left led in the proper direction, but he chose it and pressed forth.

# Chapter 2

The Somesul Mic River, more often just termed the Somes River, flowed from the northern countryside. It originated in the Apuseni Mountains and wandered through the surrounding forested hills and farmlands and eventually entered Cluj. At the outer parts of the city, the Somes journeyed at ground level. As it streamed through the old city center, it passed through a lichen-covered stone canal several meters below the ground level. It was not a large river; rarely more than seventy feet wide, and certainly not deep enough to support boats of any kind. In almost all sections a person could wade across, although this was an event seldom seen.

Unfortunately, some people heartlessly considered the Somes a waste deposit site. On certain sections of its banks, green and blue plastic bottles and bags aggregated. Despite this, the river still flowed steadily, and did proudly maintain much of its charm.

John wandered along the river each day. He started in the city center and traveled westward, letting the river guide him through various sections of Cluj. One attribute of the Somes River that had immediately caught John's attention was the fishermen relaxing upon its banks. Most were elderly men, with long wooden fishing poles, and most fished alone. They set their poles on small "y" shaped pieces of oak, and then reclined and leisurely consumed the bags of seeds that inevitably accompanied them. They would arrive early morning and at dusk would vanish, but they were sure to return the next day.

What fascinated John about these fishermen was the issue of fish. Never had he seen a fish in the Somes. He had positioned himself on its small bridges and studied the water numerous times, and he had inspected the river as he walked along its banks, but not once had he spotted a single fish. Even observing the fishermen from a distance, he had never seen one of them pull a fish from the cold waters.

It was around eleven on a sunny Monday as John walked through the Parcul Central towards the Somes. He had noticed one particular fisherman, located by the nearby bridge, several times in the last weeks. Each time the man sat inches from the water, not moving at all; he appeared petrified, a work of art chiseled from granite. The river seemed to transfix him. John conjectured he was in his seventies, but it was difficult to decipher the ages of the fishermen as their countenances were tanned and wrinkled from innumerable hours in the sun.

The previous time John had walked by him this stationary position altered. The fisherman had moved; in fact, John believed he might have nodded to him as he passed. Of this he was unsure, and as he recalled he began to question his memory and soundness, but yes, he believed he had nodded. And if so, perhaps the opportunity to converse had arisen. He wanted to ask about life by the river. What in heavens did this fisherman think about while spending the entire day alone by the flowing water? And John wanted to know if he had ever reeled in a fish.

Upon reaching the Strada Independentei, John strolled westward along the Somes. Grassy banks unfolded to his right, col-
lapsing at the bottom into the water. Maple trees lined these banks
and their leaves had just begun to vein crimson and yellow. As he
neared the bridge, he spotted the aged fisherman. He hesitated.
Why not proceed? In fairness, he contrived numerous reasons,
some quite compelling, most quite inane, but he chose to disre-
gard them. Hopping off the sidewalk, he descended the bank, and
sat facing the water. The ground was moist, as the blades of grass
still cradled the morning fog. The fisherman was no more than
twenty feet away, masticating on sunflower seeds.

The situation could be accurately described as awkward. He
did not want to directly approach the fisherman for fear of distressing him, so he sat in silence and sought some sign. John faced him
several times, hoping their eyes would meet, but the fisherman's
eyes met only rushing water. He seemed content, for he had his
full bag of seeds and the sunlight was streaming. Reclining on his
lower back, he adjusted his fishing pole every fifteen minutes.

After an hour passed, it was time to depart. This venture has
failed miserably. John stood and climbed towards the sidewalk, his
feet slipping on the slick grass. Turning for a final peek, he noticed
that he had sat up. The fisherman, with narrow eyes to begin with,
squinted in the sunlight and nodded at John. John reciprocated
with several nods and was uncertain how to proceed, yet found
himself descending towards him.

He stood about seven feet away but the fisherman had now
turned to the river. John's fingers slid across the stubble on his jaw.
The fisherman wasn't going to turn back. He needed something interesting to say, but admittedly, it had been a while since the need
arose to conjure up something compelling. "How's the fishing?"
John inquired. He instantly rued the question, wondering if a more
banal query were indeed possible. The fisherman spit out shell

and held the bag towards John. He hesitated, then moved forward and dipped his hand into the bag, pulling out a handful of seeds. Several fell through his fingers onto the grass and he checked the fisherman's reaction but he remained impassive. John sat facing the water and sampling the heavily salted seeds, rapidly discovering that he struggled to separate seed and shell in his mouth. He lacked the fisherman's experience. How challenging could it be? He began spitting out and swallowing various amalgams of shell and seed. The fisherman was aware of this, for the right edge of his mouth turned up in amusement.

After half an hour, the fisherman removed a baguette sandwich from a leather satchel and ripped a piece from it, holding it out to John. He received it and thanked him. Now John did not want this sandwich, but declining was not an option, so at least knowing what comprised it might be helpful. Yet opening and inspecting might also be impertinent, so he blindly bit and chewed what tasted like deeply smoked meat and stale bread. The fisherman observed him, and finally spoke, his voice little more than a whisper. Alas, John had not paid attention to the words, just their soft sound, and after a protracted period of silence the fisherman repeated his question, asking if he liked the food. John, swallowing the unyielding bread, said yes, he liked it very much.

The grass around them heated in the sunlight. The fisherman lay back facing the sky, and John turned to the river. The water bubbled over rocks nearby, but ran in smooth sheets in other sections. A red soda can floated past, and memories surfaced of his last days in Manhattan, seven months ago, before departing for Europe. He had watched the Hudson River in all its vastness flow by. His final days there were spent alone, crestfallen and wearing his unlaundered business suits and gazing at the water from downtown benches. The river, despite existing alongside millions of people, was surprisingly tranquil.

John now reclined on the warm grass, minding the sky and considering these last seven months. He had wandered through many countries throughout Europe before choosing to halt in Romania five months ago. Here was a land that was once so vibrant, so attractive, and then had been devastated by communism. But they had freed themselves from that regime just a few years ago, and now were struggling to navigate, struggling to form an identity. These last months had dissolved without John's noticing.

Only two clouds, moving briskly, were present amongst the azure above. The sunlight gradually warmed his forehead and cheeks. He closed his eyes, listened to the water gurgling over stones, and was thankful everything seemed so far away.

# Chapter 3

Alina checked her watch before turning the doorknob to enter. It was seven o'clock plus two minutes. Her grandmother would be waiting inside and the topic of time would inevitably be raised.

Her left index finger, thin and wrinkled, tapped the plastic tabletop, producing the lone sound in the apartment. She sat on a metal chair, her white slippers beside her. "It's not six-thirty anymore," the old woman said from her seat as Alina stepped inside the apartment. Her finger was now motionless.

"And how are you feeling?" Alina inquired in a hearty tone.

She stared at Alina. "Terrible."

Alina removed a glass from the cupboard. When she rotated the worn faucet knobs, the pipes rattled and groaned for several seconds from deep inside the walls. Two rapid explosions of rust colored water proceeded, followed by a steady stream of slightly clearer fluid. She filled her glass and sat across from her grandmother.

"It's not six-thirty," her grandmother said. "It's past seven now."

"Would you like to have something to eat?" Alina said.

"Of course I prepared you something. The food was ready over half an hour ago."

Her grandmother, wiry and with a full head of white hair, arose swiftly as her nightgown ruffled, and she kicked her bare feet into slippers. Thin blue veins webbed beneath her skin, which had become translucent from years of staying indoors. She removed a plate of chicken from the oven, rearranged four slices of boiled potato next to the meat, and laid the plate in front of Alina. Her legs were spread widely and her hands posted on her hips as she stared at Alina and the food.

Alina, versed with this routine from her weekly visits, abstained from making any requests. She would have preferred if her grandmother sat down instead of hovering over her, but she knew her grandmother was aware she preferred this, and thus would certainly refrain from doing so. So she ate the cold chicken and potatoes in silence and without looking away from the plate.

"You can come here any time you want," her grandmother said. Alina sipped from her glass and rolled the tinny water around her mouth. "You don't just have to crash into here once a month or whatever you do."

"The chicken is very good," Alina said. She consumed the final piece on her plate, and chewed the undercooked potatoes while her grandmother tracked the motion of her fork. As she pierced the last potato slice her grandmother snatched the plate and dropped it into the sink. After the groaning beyond the walls, the water spurted and she scrubbed the plate, displaying her false teeth with each stroke. Alina glanced at her watch. She had to remain at least a few more minutes to minimize the ineluctable drama engendered by her departure.

"So what is happening with men?" her grandmother asked as she toweled the plate. She was not looking at Alina.

"How do I know how their gender is doing?"

She halted all wiping motions. "Don't try to be clever," she said. "Are you at least with a suitor now?"

Alina's jaw muscles bulged. "As I've said before, I'm too busy with work at the moment."

Her grandmother inserted the plate in the plastic drying rack and sat down. "Work is fine. But you are thirty-seven years old."

"So I am."

"Don't have a fresh mouth," she said. "You are thirty-seven. Thirty-seven. God, forgive her, I shudder to even think about it! Horrible. I was married when I was eighteen. Your mother when she was twenty. You are embarrassing yourself and your family."

Alina arose and chose to refill her glass with the metallic water rather than remain sitting beside her grandmother. "You have mentioned that a few dozen times before," she said while looking into the sink. Her grandmother did not respond. "The corporation I work for is seven days a week of work and I'm trying to get promoted. I need to dedicate the time."

"Well we didn't have all these corporations or whatever nonsense in this country in my time. But women did know how to get a husband and make a family." She scanned Alina's profile, probing for some reaction. "Nothing is more rewarding than that."

Alina sipped the water while staring into the murkiness of the drain. "I'm sure."

"Don't have a fresh mouth."

"Times have altered. Now we have some free markets here. Opportunities might soon be opening."

Her grandmother stood. "Perhaps. But those high positions are for men." She moved to Alina's side by the sink. "It's OK for you to work a little, but you will never succeed, and only be depressed your whole life without a husband. Nothing is more important than that. All that fancy studying you did and whatever this work you do is ruining your life." She brought a package over and popped the plastic open. Alina removed a biscuit, and her grandmother demanded she take another.

"I should be going now."

Her grandmother slammed the biscuits on the counter, shattering several. "Do something worthwhile for once. You're still attractive. All the men always liked you. But they won't be interested forever." She moved closer, her eyes narrowing. "Soon, at your age, you'll be lucky to find anyone."

Alina faced her grandmother, observing her quivering lips hungrily anticipating a response. "If I find someone with the proper mentality, I might make the time and become interested in him," she said, aware of her comment's provocative nature.

"Don't you get so fancy or picky," her grandmother said, shoving the biscuits across the counter. "Those men were fine for me and your mother. Don't get so fancy."

Alina thanked her grandmother for the meal. She said she would see her next week. The ruddiness of grandmother's face instantly drained, and she silently offered the biscuits. Alina received a shard of one, kissing her grandmother on the cheek as she departed. She peeked back inside. Her grandmother was sitting at the table staring at the bare refrigerator door.

# Chapter 4

He had ignored several calls from him that morning. When his phone had rung four minutes ago, John finally answered, agreeing to meet a desperate sounding Patrick at the Café Latte that afternoon at three. For Patrick to sound harried was not novel, and normally nothing of momentous urgency elicited this desperation, but John agreed to meet him nonetheless. The café, perhaps the most expensive in Cluj, was located by the Piata Unirii, and had a terrace on the sidewalk overlooking the bustling square and the ancient, gothic St. Mihai's Cathedral. It was not a café John cared for, but the view was splendid and it was Patrick's favorite locale, so he conceded to the meeting.

The day was the coolest in the last weeks. The vague breeze forecasted the harsher autumn weather descending onto Cluj. John wore jeans and a woolen turtleneck sweater. As he neared the café and surveyed the tables, he observed numerous heads adorned with sunglasses, all staring into the passing crowd, all craving to be noticed. One of those pairs of oversized sunglasses must be perched upon Patrick's lengthy nose. An arm frenetically waved and John's name was yelled at a high pitch.

Patrick arose and pulled a black iron chair from the table as John approached. He smiled unabashedly, and encapsulated John's hand with both of his while shaking vigorously. John mentioned his reaction might befit those who hadn't seen each other for four or five years, but it had only been six days. He added that they had only known each other for a month as well. Patrick's cheeks reddened as they sat. On the table was a coffee, its black surface trembling from the activity. John requested a bottle of local merlot wine from the young waiter when Patrick, gasping, interrupted the order. The waiter silently stared at the base of the table, his dark hair fastidiously gelled to the side.

"What's this nonsense?" John asked.

"Do not drink the poison in this country that they call wine."

"That poison treats me quite well."

Patrick shook his head side to side as he looked at his gleaming shoes. "I know you are a highly cultured man, although you are intent on feigning otherwise," he said. "In my satchel I have a Bordeaux, from a vineyard bordering on my family's country estate. This bottle is ours to enjoy."

The iron of the chair fitted the curve of John's back. "That is heartening to hear. But for now, while sitting at this establishment, I will manage partaking of the aforementioned toxins."

Patrick, ignoring John, handed the waiter a fold of cash and told him to bring glasses and a bottle opener. The waiter promptly nodded as the cash seamlessly melded into his back pocket, and he returned moments later, departing only when Patrick stated his presence was no longer required. Patrick smoothed the sleeves of his cotton blazer and rearranged his scarf. Caressing the bottle with his right hand, he offered it to John, who received it on his fingertips. He studied the label: Chateau Palmer, appellation Margaux, twelve years old. Patrick's moist eyes were fixed upon him.

"You have something lovely here," John said.

"I knew you would appreciate it," Patrick said. "I knew you would understand."

John avoided eye contact and suggested an opening of the bottle. Patrick effortlessly removed the cork and allowed the wine to breathe.

"I wanted to ask your advice about..." Patrick began softly.

"Ask me what?" John interrupted.

Patrick hesitated. "About investing funds in certain American corporate bonds."

John studied the tanned stones of the cathedral's lofty clock tower across the street. "Why ask me?"

"Don't be ridiculous."

"I'm trying not to be. I don't keep up with the markets anymore."

"Don't be ridiculous. You were a wizard."

A young couple passed the café, laughing together. They held hands as they walked. The numerous sunglass-covered heads in the café sedulously tracked their path, hoping at least one would turn and notice them.

"I don't keep up anymore. You're best seeking advice elsewhere." The cork, lying beside him, was blood colored.

Patrick leaned forward and scoffed, while proudly stroking his wine bottle. "I have gleaned that you had immense success in New York," he said. He waived his hands around him. "And here you are now in distant Romania doing nothing. I don't profess to know why, but I can sense your abilities."

The pavement was charcoal beneath their feet. "And here you are," John said, waiving his hand in a corresponding manner, "having accepted a post at this university, teaching various language courses when you certainly had far more lucrative opportunities back in France." Patrick looked away, focusing on the pedestrians. "As you had mentioned, half of your family is in the banking industry in France. Yet you left, or shall I say, with due reverence towards veracity, you fled."

As Patrick's teeth grinded, they fell silent.

Regardless of his disposition, which at the moment was not particularly convivial, Patrick would never interrupt the formalities of his beloved wine ritual. He dexterously poured a bit of wine into John's glass and waited, motionless. John swirled the dark fluid. He breathed the wine and sipped. As it spread across his tongue he was reminded of the complexity and dimensions that certain well-crafted wines can possess, and he nodded his assent. Patrick filled both glasses, and they drank and absorbed surrounding sounds: the griping of struggling car engines and the tinny laughter from specious conversations. They remained silent. Patrick had not been pleased with John's prior comments, and John wasn't overly enamored with Patrick's intrusions either.

John never postulated that it could happen, but yes, he was actually assuaged by the sight of Cosmin sauntering along the sidewalk, for he knew he would join them at the table and perchance offer some relief from their disagreeable moment. Yet Patrick was not fond of company unless he had done the inviting. After noticing John waving, Cosmin shuffled through the crowd to their table and sat, exhaling fervently, between them. Patrick didn't move; his expression was glaciated in aversion.

"How are you my friend?" Cosmin asked John.

"This is Patrick."

Cosmin lifted his eyebrows substantially as he turned to Patrick, in a wretched attempt to suggest his presence was just noticed. An extended arm accompanied his hello. The greeting was reciprocated with a listless handshake. While Cosmin inquired about what region of France he derived from, he turned to the bottle of wine, and Patrick watched in horror as he raised the bottle inches from his face and studied the label. Cosmin apparently had not noticed or cared that Patrick failed to respond to his question. "This appears fine," Cosmin said, "very fine." Patrick sipped his wine and looked askance. Cosmin ached for a glassful, but wanted it to be offered. He lacked the courage to pour it himself, and was too proud to ask. He requested John's opinion on the vintage, hoping the response would serve as a bridge to his obtaining a serving, but he received no answer. The silence was interrupted as Cosmin rambled to Patrick about his current doctoral studies in European history, and he revealed his biting opinions concerning episodes in French annals. His ensuing lecture was uniform: he only discussed events where France suffered deleterious consequences or ignominy, and then explained why France deserved better or was misunderstood. In between these points, he invariably inserted anecdotes referring to his lofty academic standing, and work as a teacher's assistant lecturing allegedly attentive classes.

John had refilled his glass and now watched the customers at the café as Cosmin's voice persisted in the background. This café had some of the highest prices in the city. Cluj did not have inordinate amounts of people with excess money, but this was one of the locales where those who did, or more often those wanting to feign that they did, assembled. Despite plentiful customers, only two waiters were present. It was uncommon in Romania to have more than one or two waitpersons, regardless of the size of the establishment or demand of the clients. More than that had been considered a waste of money, and this philosophy remained intact without scrutiny. Two women in their twenties, both possibly attractive but certainly not indisposed to employing vast amounts of makeup, sat at the next table. Their cocktail glasses were empty, yet no waiter inquired if they wanted more. From their frequent glares towards the inside of the establishment it was evident that they sought service. Yet they refused, heavens forbid, to stand up, and no one attended to them, and the situation remained unchanged.

"An excellent vintage."

John turned and Cosmin gazed at his glass. He hadn't yielded in his quest for a sampling. His discourse, not surprisingly, had proved ineffective in inducing the beneficence of Patrick, for Patrick once again savored his wine and Cosmin remained bereft of drink. He was pressing John to intercede and request the extra glass, but as the bottle was Patrick's, John left that decision to him.

"Have you noticed how little attention the customers receive?" John said.

Cosmin looked at the tables around him and gradually smiled. "That is all they need."

"The cafe could be receiving far more orders."

Cosmin laughed. "People are not used to attention around here. Ceausescu's regime collapsed a few years ago, but as you have seen, not much changed."

Patrick watched them forlornly. He was not a gregarious sort, but with the few people he did associate with, he talked ceaselessly. John was among those, although John intuited never to inquire anything about Patrick's private time, as Patrick never raised the topic. Cosmin was just an intrusion. John had not expected him to be overjoyed with Cosmin's presence, but Cosmin had been recruited to alleviate the discomfort and he was not successful; he had exacerbated it. As John stroked his chin observing Patrick wallow in silence, he decided it would be best if Cosmin departed.

"So where are you going now?" John asked Cosmin.

Cosmin turned to John, stupefied. He believed his stay had just begun, and besides, he had yet to inveigle a sampling of the fine vintage.

"I assume you were headed somewhere."

"Well in a while I was considering meeting with friends in Grigorescu," Cosmin said. "In a while," he quickly added.

"Excellent. I have no doubt I'll hear from you later."

"Certainly I could stay for a bit."

"No need. But I have no doubt I'll hear from you later."

Cosmin resigned, patting his thighs and standing. He said goodbye to Patrick by complimenting the newest French railway system. After shaking John's hand, he weaved his way through to the sidewalk.

"Amicable display you put on," John said.

Patrick appeared scandalized. "What are you saying?"

"I believe I was clear."

He bounteously refilled their glasses in an attempt to palliate John's impression. Patrick stated how arduous it could be for both of them, coming from their distant countries, to adjust to this environment, and he listed numerous faults with the city and businesses and people. He frequently mentioned the supposed faults of all the countries he had visited.

"I assume your work contract here is not difficult to break," John said, "and you could return home immediately." Patrick's supple hands rapidly primped his burgundy silk scarf. He offered no retort.

The time had arrived to ease the situation. "Either way, sometimes it is essential to be far away," John said.

"Yes," Patrick said, enlivening. He looked at John. "That is quite true. Quite true."

# Chapter 5

To reach her office door Alina had to pass the cubicles; a dozen were packed together in the room. Sounds of retching printers and discontented voices filled the air. This path to her office was formidable. She had worked in one of these cubicles two years ago, before her promotion to the position of assistant director with private office and window. She thus knew most of the cubicle inhabitants, and many would attempt to stop her and gossip interminably about the company. An unobstructed trek to her office was what she sought. This was not effortlessly obtained.

Of course particular methods to eschew these conversations had evolved. Her prime technique was to focus on work papers as she walked, never looking away. In actuality she analyzed them, for there was no reason to squander the work opportunity, but even on the rare occasion when a blank sheet was before her she never averted her eyes. Certainly traversing this way increased the chance for collisions, but over the years she had honed this technique and could now negotiate a labyrinth without looking up. Unfortunately, the few who would still attempt to initiate conversation were also those with no regard for her diligence, and thus were the ones she least wanted to converse with.

"Alina!"

Her neck muscles tensed. She paused before looking up from her statistical sheet covering property value fluctuations in southwest Bucharest. The voice's origin was no surprise. Voicu's head was jutting from his cubicle's entrance. He rocked on his rolling chair, his light, thin hair carefully parted to the side.

"Yes?"

"It's really unbelievable what I heard," he said, mouth agape. Alina's lack of response was distressing; he would amplify the drama. "This rumor, it relates to you." He frantically surveyed her, assessing whether his latest utterance was more effective at eliciting interest than his initial venture. It was not, but to limit the duration of this interaction, she responded: "Nice."

He cupped his left hand and beckoned her to come closer. She arrived at his cubicle. He licked his upper lip and peered left and right, an act of questionable consequence, since he was now within the cubicle and was viewing blank walls three feet from his face.

"I heard the vice-president of the company is resigning," he said, maintaining eye contact, "and that you might be considered for the position." He stretched his stunted body and smiled triumphantly.

"Voicu, I have heard nothing about this."

"Yes, but I heard…" he began, but Alina interrupted him by raising her index finger and stating she had work. She walked away, focused on her statistics. Her black shoes, purchased a week ago and a bit tight, made no sound on the carpeted floor. Most office rumors were baseless. Yet, slightly abashed, she could not prevent wondering about this one. She knew the vice-president, Andre Brancusi, had personal problems, but the details were vague. Could he be leaving? Even if he was, Vlad was above her; he was the head director. People were already shocked at her promotion to an assistant director. It was uncommon for women in this part of the world to occupy this position in a company.

It would be prudent if she refrained from ruminating on the possibility of this promotion: she yearned for it far too much, and it would inevitably lead to anxiety and then to a burning frustration. Yes, it would be best to ignore the subject. But could he be leaving? If he did, would the company's president consider her for the position? Though he was a distant man, he undoubtedly knew she was the most capable. He had consulted with her directly several times. She had been promoted initially because she accomplished tasks at twice the speed of her colleagues, and everyone consulted her when plagued with grave work dilemmas. Even Vlad asked her to his office, albeit discreetly, to help him with intricate issues, but of course never did he mention her contributions once the problems were solved. Oh, he was quite careful about that. Yes, she was the most capable. But promotion to the level of vice-president unfortunately required more than possessing sublime abilities.

Both her hands pushed the office door shut. She squinted as afternoon sunlight poured into her absurdly tiny room. Stepping past her desk, which occupied most of the space, she pressed her forehead against the window. The Somes flowed several stories below. The glass was cold on her skin and she closed her eyes; it soothed and penetrated deeply. How long did she remain in that position?

The surface of her desk was polished with a crisp lemon scent. She kept the spray and napkins in her bottom drawer. All paperwork and office supplies were tidily filed. She typed and the phone rang.

"I need you to stop by my office," Vlad said.

"I'm in the middle of handling a project," Alina said. "I'll be there in fifteen minutes."

"Make it sooner."

What did Vlad want now? Just yesterday she had helped him with the figures from Sibiu. She was inundated with her own work and he was supposed to be the head director. Perhaps she bore the title of assistant director, but she possessed a far more complete comprehension of company projects and in what manner they were best dealt with. She didn't need to be bothered by Vlad now. After five minutes she ceased working and exited her office, knocking on the door down the hall.

"Yes?"

Alina entered. Vlad was behind his desk speaking on the phone. As he laughed, he leaned forward revealing the circle of pale flesh capping his skull. A few malnourished hairs had been plastered across this tundra in a miserable attempt to conceal it. He did not look at Alina but forced another laugh, which was too loud and extended to have faith in its authenticity. She sat in front of his desk scratching notes onto her papers before her. The phone hit the receiver.

He stared at her; she waited.

"How is Bucharest?" he asked.

"Mediocre. Little change, but not surprising. Real estate..."

"They are foolish," he interrupted.

"Who?"

He repositioned himself, lifting a mug and stridently slurping. Even if the coffee were boiling in the cup, it didn't warrant that level of sound. "The Farcou Company, I just got off the phone with, " he said. "Foolish." She didn't respond. "I am the one who provided them funding in the beginning. They were two people working in an apartment before I approved of our investment. I got them their status. I did." He shook his head. Alina was about to redirect the discussion back to Bucharest property values. "And I can take away my support any time," Vlad continued. "But they

33

fail to appreciate that. Now they're looking to move beyond our services."

"That was inevitable," Alina said. "They need to expand as well."

Vlad glared at her. "What they need is to know I can ruin them."

The ensuing silence was not pleasurable. "Do you have something you want me to review? I must get back."

Vlad placed the cup on the desk and leaned forward. The springs in his chair creaked. "I hear things are serious with Andre."

"Let's hope he is fine."

Vlad stood, the springs noisily expanding. In the corner of the office a coffee pot percolated. He poured while staring at Alina and the black liquid spilled onto his hand, inducing a violent jerking and a stream of bitter vociferations. Someone was knocking softly on the door, but he paid no attention. "My guess," he said, his hand convulsing, "is that Cristi will be choosing a replacement for Andre soon."

Alina placed her pen upon the papers in her lap.

Vlad scanned her face. "I certainly have done much for the company," he said, continuing to monitor her.

"I'm sure."

The knocking had stopped.

"You help Cristi occasionally," Vlad said, his eyes slits. "You've been by his office several times."

"I do what the company needs."

"Of course," Vlad said, displaying teeth and wresting a laugh. "I have assigned you to do much around here. And I was the one who approved of your promotion to assistant director." He rested his fingertips on the desk. "I got you to where you are."

She watched his lower lip twitch. "So do you need my help now? I need to return." She was acutely aware of the incendiary nature of her question, but could not resist.

"*I* need your help? What the hell is that supposed to mean?" He sneered. "Why would *I* be needing your help?"

He normally, in various veiled forms and behind a sealed door, asked her to help him solve problems or advise him at least once a day. That was the minimum.

"So are *you* needing my help with anything?" he said.

Not a single instance existed where he had helped her, nor did he possess the acumen to do so. "No," she said. "Anything else?"

As he leaned forward, stroking the stubble on his neck, the blue veins intersecting the desolate real estate atop his skull distended. "You can leave."

She departed and rapidly returned to her office. The glass was cool on her forehead.

# Chapter 6

John walked Strada Horea towards the northern part of Cluj on a Thursday afternoon in late October. White light filtered through the omnipresent clouds. The crisp air did not penetrate the woolen turtleneck sweater he had purchased two weeks ago at a local market. Pressing his palm against the front of the sweater, he smiled gently. Each Sunday, vendors filed into Cluj from the countryside and set up tables near the Piata Mihai Viteazul. Various goods were sold, from animal skins to handmade clothing to used plumbing and household products. The initial price the vendors demanded for goods was never the sensible price and was rarely accepted, perhaps only by those too shy or too proud to bargain. John was not indisposed to bargaining; in fact, he enjoyed it. He relished immersing himself in the strategy involved.

When he had approached the table covered with the woolen sweaters on a cool Sunday two weeks ago, an elderly woman, her head adorned by a white cloth with embroidered tulips, arose from a crate behind the table and demanded to know how many articles of clothing he was troubling her for. She had picked up her thick body with surprising speed and was sure not to look directly at him. He ignored her charming question and examined the sweaters, careful to keep them neatly folded, for he did not want to provide her a tangible reason to be riled; at least not yet. He found a dour, gray sweater to his liking and inquired about the price.

"Fifty lei," she said.

John shook his head side to side and returned the sweater onto the pile. She didn't move. The inflated price was not belied by her rehearsed, somber expression. He chose the same sweater, of a different shade, and asked.

"Forty-five lei."

John again shook his head, this time relinquishing a note of disgust. He wanted the gray sweater and would pay a maximum of thirty lei. She wanted at least forty, but unfortunately for her, customers in the market were sparse. He stood directly before her and unhurriedly turned his head left and right, inspecting the relatively quiet market. She watched him, but would not turn her head to acknowledge his revealing survey.

Taking two steps away from the table, he fumbled in his pocket, removing two ten lei notes. He had a total of eighty lei in his pocket, divided between six ten lei notes, and four five lei notes. He raised the gray sweater and extended the twenty lei near to her pursed features; proximate enough so she could sniff the paper. Her nostrils did tremble, but she motioned him away with a dismissive slapping of the air, while scoffing and staring at the dusty sidewalk. He sighed animatedly and returned the sweater.

When a man about fifty years old approached the left side of the table she darted to that area, zealously attending to him. She was absolutely delighted to ignore John, delivering the message that his trivial fiscal offers had deemed him irrelevant and, judging by her slight grin, worthless as well. She didn't even bother to glance at him again, even though he stood next to the table and ruffled sweaters. Sadly for her, the man abruptly departed, and she was left in the awkward position of staring at the empty space where moments ago her deliverance had stood, the recipient of her fawning.

She was too proud to move, but too much humiliation, caused by her ensnarement, would lead her to anger and ultimately to irrationality. John broke the stalemate by coughing and dropping a sweater behind the table. She returned and scooped it off the ground, slamming it back onto the surface and scolding him to be more careful. He fumbled for fifteen seconds in his pocket, feigning an industrious search for more money. After glancing down, he removed a five lei note, and now offered the twenty-five lei. She shook her head and grunted no, although the intensity of her revulsion had clearly abated. Success was near, but a slight mishap could extinguish the deal.

He sighed, then straightened suddenly, as if some realization had dawned upon him. Her jaw tensed. He thrust his hand into his other pocket, immediately clutching another five lei note he had placed there. She was not facing him but did a commendable job of covertly peeking. Yet he continued the motions of searching for money while wearing varying irritated expressions, acting as if no currency could be located. She was motionless, watching the ground beside his feet and keeping him peripherally visible. Eventually he removed the five lei note, smiling in triumph. He presented thirty lei before her. It vanished from his hand with admirable speed. He lifted the gray sweater and departed, rubbing the fleecy material between his fingertips.

That sweater now served him well in the blustery conditions as he walked down the Strada Horea. The scenery began to change. He was still proximate enough to the city center that the majority of the buildings were of the older, ornate architecture he found entrancing. As he traveled north, they began to unpleasantly alter.

On both sides of the street appeared, with increasing frequency, the two or three story cement structures constructed during communist times, many covered with plastic signs from the foundering ground floor shops. Aesthetics had not been a dominating factor in their design.

A block and a half from the train station he saw them coming; nothing could be done. Three children, wearing ragged adults' clothing, scuttled around him. The tallest extended his arm with his muddied palm facing the bland sky. His left eye was bloodshot. They encircled him and began chanting. Their dark hair flew in all directions, and the creases in their faces, accentuated by their verbal escapade, were filled with grease. They wanted money. John ignored them and continued to walk, but the circle around him was maintained. He was the nucleus, and remarkably the radius never varied, as they had honed this activity.

Months ago, when he had first arrived in Cluj, he gave money to such groups of begging children. They were primarily gypsies. He possessed little knowledge about them, but soon discovered that many gypsy families lived apart from society, outside the laws of the state. Their children often didn't attend schools, and plenty of the adults were not part of the tax-paying economy. Many labored in the countryside and brought produce to the city, and others were involved with illegally procuring and vending goods. In the center of the city, near the major piatas, older gypsy men, pirouetting their mustaches, would approach John and whip freshly acquired watches or necklaces out from under their leather coats and whisper prices.

John, when he had first encountered a group of children begging for money, could not resist and gave a generous amount. He did the same several more times. But the reward for his benevolence was being hunted and plagued with heightened intensity. They would pursue John into a store, or enter a café and surround his table, even if he was sitting with others. After he reached into his pockets and gave money, they screeched for more. Cosmin had told him that information travels among gypsies with alarming rapidity; they knew who in the city gave and targeted those people. He lectured that nothing should be given, that the adults who sent the children out hoarded all the money, and that John was headed for trouble. John was surprised, and perhaps not as much by the mounting onslaught but rather that Cosmin's discourse actually seemed valid.

Fortunately, the gypsy children were also economical in their efforts and would not dissipate energy begging from unyielding sources, so John had decided to stop donating. Accordingly, they would ignore him. Alas, his tidy solution was not summarily effective. He was now amidst a transition phase. They still apparently hoped, despite his ignoring them several times, that he could be cajoled back into relinquishing funds.

The chanting and moaning persisted as he walked and the darkened palm thrust back and forth. Physical contact was normally eschewed, but John felt the lengthy fingernails clamping into his forearm. Pedestrians glanced at the situation, and then looked down at the cracked sidewalk. It was difficult for John to refrain from looking at these gypsies, for their odd-pitched moans tempted one to observe the source, but John knew any eye contact would instantly fortify their vigor. He passed the front of the train station, eyes fixed ahead, struggling to avoid peering at them. Finally their circle snapped, and they darted single file through a rusted side door of the station.

The pedestrian bridge that passed over a side canal in the northern part of the city would not win architectural accolades. It was narrow, bare metal, with sharpened railings on both sides. The scene below, a thin canal replete with muddy water sloughing by, did not allay any discomfort engendered by the sight of the bridge. John had sequestered himself in the old city center for his first months and rarely left that area, but lately he had considered venturing to other parts of the city, and he now descended the bridge's stairs into the unexplored Dambul Rotund district.

It was mid-afternoon and the sky was alabaster. The cumbersome cloud blanket above seemed permanently fastened. John traveled down the first road he encountered, which ran parallel to the canal, with no destination in mind. A metal fence stood to his left, with more of its sections absent then present. In the openings he observed an empty parched lot, and beside it a five story building with gray, stained walls: a factory of some sort. Conveyor belts extended from several entrances, with dozens of metal tubs dangling along their tracks. He recalled similar contraptions in cement factories in the United States.

Something was peculiar about this scene. Several minutes passed, and he was both unsure and troubled why he had not noticed earlier, but he finally realized what it was: there was no one, not a single person in the lot or walking around the factory or on the street. Clumps of dark weed patches sagged on the sides of the road. A lone car was in front of the factory but would not be driving away anytime soon due to its dearth of tires and an engine. The factory windows consisted of hundreds of square glass panels, mostly shattered or missing. Below him a hubcap, with a thistle plant growing through its rusted holes, lay askew on a rock.

He continued down the road as it curved closer to the canal. The sour tang of sewage encumbered the air. A similar factory followed, this one perhaps narrower and with faded blue garbage bins lining its side. The parking area was deserted, as not even a plundered vehicle occupied a space. Possibly the contents of the bins might divulge something about the location. John strode across the lot, glancing left and right, worried, or possibly hoping, someone might howl at him, branding him a trespasser, but of course only silence. Inside the bin he found only a heavy layer of dust and a brown plastic bottle, likely a beer bottle, but time and exposure to the elements had effaced the label. In the other bin he noticed a broken plank, and then what appeared to be a doll: a tiny naked doll, yellowed and lying on its back amidst the dust. Returning across the lot, the former unease of pending castigation vanished, and only the stillness remained.

Some activity or life must be present. He pressed forth along the street, passing one factory after another, scanning the landscape. They varied little in size and shape and were identical in their condition: abandoned. The wind, suddenly arising, was burdened with coarse red dust carrying a metallic odor. One or two business closings were fathomable, but the entire area was solitude. And where was everybody? Atop a small hill he gazed back at the row of forsaken buildings. The desolation was inexplicably compelling. He continued to stare, squinting as the heavy wind whisked by. Finally, he coughed dryly and turned away.

The road sloped downward, and when it leveled he happened upon a cluster of apartments. They were identical squat, rectangular buildings, painted with formerly blue and white stripes, which now, through aging and grime, had formed one vapid hue. A string hung across the yard from which an assortment of clothing and rags dangled. He stared at an aggregation of undergarments.

For the first time in what seemed decades, he heard voices. Nobody was apparent, but sounds emanated from somewhere inside the apartments or hallways. Tiny parking areas separated one building from the next. The pavement was riddled with cracks. Below him, the roots of a maple tree had broken through the sidewalk. He sat on a plastic crate beneath the tree, unsure what prompted him to do so, for he was not fatigued and the view was far from resplendent. Scratching his shoe against the sidewalk, he grasped that he wanted to see people, any people.

These last months he had spent much time alone. He did his best to keep his apartment sealed, and when he ventured out, he was usually alone. The bustling environment of his days in New York was a past he could no longer conceive. His current solitude was precisely what he had been seeking, for he didn't want to host his grievous memories in the company of others. Everyone in his past had thought him content, even joyous, but his life had only been barren for as long as he could remember. He possessed a desolate soul.

He had decided he must cross the ocean. He would cross the ocean to meander through Europe in an attempt to live a quiet and isolated life, and perhaps discover what was absent inside of him. He wandered through numerous countries, and after entering Romania he sensed a country struggling to recover, a land where mystery still abounded; he felt a certain connection and was intrigued. In Cluj he found the wine plentiful and cheap, he could read countless books with few interruptions, and living undetected could be accomplished with ease. He chose to remain for a while, and months dissipated rapidly. And he detected little change within himself. Yes, his hollow past tormented him while in the company of others, but lamentably it was also intolerable alone. What a lovely quandary. Now, impulsively, at least for the moment, and for the first time in months, he needed to see evidence of life.

A brown leaf, orange-streaked, landed on his thigh. Above, the branches were dark outlines against the bleakness. The colors of the intact leaves were not evident as the sky's white light bleached everything of its vibrancy. A sudden grating sound jerked his eyes forward. A lone can, crushed in its middle, was traversing the parking lot, its sporadic journey powered by the mercurial wind. John found himself rooting for the can's successful crossing to the languid weed patches waiting silently on the side, but the can halted midway and failed to move again.

If not for Cosmin invading John's apartment several nights a week and occasionally dragging him out, and Patrick's daily calls of which John answered once every three or four days, he knew he would have interacted with no one. What possible reason was there to venture out? Cheap wine tasted the same in his living room as in the city, and in his room he did not have to face questions: Why did he leave New York? Why was he here? Why did he reveal so little? Even he didn't know all the answers. His intention was not to be churlish with others, but without the "others" in the equation there was no need to be anything. Since he had arrived the days had not distinguished themselves from each other, nor the months, but he was vaguely aware of a gradual passing of time. He was not a participant of that march, but rather a detached observer, staring into the sky as life moved on everywhere but within himself.

They were in the parking lot. He missed their entrance, but a young woman, at most in her late teens and pushing a stroller, traipsed with an older, heavier version of herself. Both wore faded sweatpants and sneakers devoid of laces. They were speaking, but the words were inaudible. Their pace was so sluggish it seemed they paused after each step. No one walks that laggardly without reason, John considered. This walk, they did not want it to end. The young woman tended to the silent inhabitant of the stroller while the older woman observed. These two must be a mother and daughter out for a confiding. This was probably their sole outing for the day, a brief walk outside those ominous apartment buildings. Then back inside that cement block, to endure whatever await-ed them. No surprise their pace would be deliberate. The older woman's thick arm reached and flexed as she emphasized certain points, and the younger woman nodded in sync. They halted and faced each other while the outstretched arm redoubled its efforts, and then their trudging recommenced. John was never noticed. He was proximate but motionless, and they passed him and continued around the building. He considered saying something, attempting conversation, but what on earth could be said? After they turned the corner, only barren space was left behind. A few minutes later a metal door slammed shut.

# Chapter 7

Alina wore an undershirt and zip-up sweater and athletic pants. Andrea wore the same. Their tennis rackets swayed at their sides as they approached the courts.

Alina enjoyed tennis, especially in October as it grew increasingly chilly. Running about in the brisk air rejuvenated her exhausted self. Sunday was the only day she had time to play. She also relished meeting Andrea, who rarely left her apartment and husband and two-year-old son. Andrea would claim she had to remain home because she had far too much to do, but Alina knew her husband was irate whenever she ventured out. He didn't permit her to have a job even though they desperately needed the money, and he instantly bemoaned the awful mess in their small and meticulously tidy apartment whenever she was about to go out and meet with friends.

A slight exception was Alina. Andrea and Alina had been friends since university, and Andrea's husband didn't seem as disconcerted when they met; at least the apartment's condition was not branded "a horrendous disaster" when she attempted to depart.

46

The tennis courts, located in the Parcul de Sport, were rented by the hour. Alina and Andrea arrived at two and the sun shone brightly in a sky with few clouds; fine weather for tennis. They did not engage in traditional matches, but merely rallied the ball, and after warming up they played individual points. The courts were surrounded by fields of overgrown grass and tall elm trees, and the plangent sound of rackets connecting with tennis balls, combined with the rustling leaves, created a tranquil atmosphere that contrasted pleasantly with Alina's office life.

After volleying shots for a time, Andrea proclaimed she was ready to play points. "Let the battle begin," she traditionally yelled. Alina laughed and awaited the serve. The serve was outside the lines, but Alina returned it. Andrea's poor swing belied her concentrated expression. Alina sprinted towards the weak shot and saw half of Andrea's court open. Finishing the point would be simple, and yes of course she considered it, but she gently stroked it directly towards Andrea. Andrea's next shot was into the net.

"You were fortunate," Andrea said, and Alina smiled.

They played for another hour, Andrea grunting and attempting extreme and futile shots at the court's edges, while Alina returned everything precisely within Andrea's range. After a final net shot by Andrea, they strode together off the court and Andrea pushed Alina with her racket. "Lucky shots," Andrea said. They looked at each other with amusement. They had been playing tennis together for fifteen years, and their play had evolved into a routine. Alina was far more agile and skilled, but she understood Andrea used tennis as a rare opportunity for venting frustration, and hence she kept play competitive. In truth, Andrea was cognizant of Alina's concessions and appreciated them, but certainly would never overtly state this.

They walked to the Parcul Central, which had an expansive central path lined with wooden benches, a convenient place to relax and observe passing activity. Alina stretched her legs and crossed her feet as she sat. This time was cathartic after the enervating week in the office. Andrea rambled about the various shapes and shades of tiles she hoped to install on her bare kitchen floor, while denouncing their inordinate costs. It would be a minimum of six months before they could consider purchasing.

A boy, still learning to walk, labored toward their bench, each step a new endeavor. His mother, who sat on a bench to their right, glanced at the boy and recommenced chatting with her friend. A patch of brown hair topped the boy's head, and his large eyes occupied a disproportionate area of his face. He noticed Alina watching, and stopped and smiled, revealing a varied landscape of tiny teeth and bare gums. He attempted to step towards Alina but stumbled, falling on the path. Alina and Andrea leapt up, and Alina raised him off the leaves. His mother remained immersed in her discussion. Alina brushed the dirt off the child's knees.

"Mihai," a voice yelled.

The child reared at the high-pitched voice of his mother and stepped in her direction. His mother nodded at Alina. Andrea wanted to sit again, but Alina asked her to continue down the path. Passing benches and onlookers, Andrea shared the latest news concerning their old classmates.

"Amelia was married in August, in Bucharest,"

"I'm surprised she was able to find someone interested," Alina said, with the corner of her mouth upturned.

"I think she was surprised," Andrea said, laughing.

Two ravens plunged from above, one inches behind the other, then arced upward toward the pale chestnut branches. Alina's stomach tightened at the impending topic.

"It was good to see her married though," Andrea said.

"Hopefully she's happy."

Andrea looked at her. "Why shouldn't she be, she finally got married."

"Good for her. But like I said, let's hope she's happy."

They marched in silence. Andrea's racket rested on her shoulder like an infantryman's rifle. "You know Amelia; never much fun. But I think she'll be kind to her husband."

"She was never much fun, that's true," Alina said. "But I hope that her husband is kind to her."

Andrea looked straight ahead. Her feet shuffled the dry leaves. "You're the last," she said.

"Oh?"

"The last in our class not to be married."

"Well I like to be on the top or bottom of lists," Alina said. "It's the middle that irks me."

Andrea halted and turned to Alina. Alina glared at her and they were silent, waiting.

"You dated Michael for four years," Andrea said.

"I did."

"And then you just left him."

"I did."

"Every woman was interested in him."

"Excellent, so he probably found someone else," Alina said.

Andrea propped her racket against her legs and positioned her hands on her hips. "I just don't want you to end up alone."

Alina looked at Andrea standing defiantly before her. She felt anger rising; Andrea raised the subject once again. It had been weeks.

"Apparently not all marriages are beneficial."

"What is that supposed to mean?" Andrea demanded, her face coloring. "What are you saying?"

As Alina surveyed the veins bulging in Andrea's neck and her despairing eyes, her anger dissipated, and the heaviness of compassion descended upon her. Andrea had been one of the finer students, ranked not far below Alina, a vigorous girl engaged in many school activities. She and Andrea had been on a mathematics club years ago when they visited other teams in the city testing their skills. Andrea had been successful, rejoicing in their victories. Now she was not even permitted to work a part-time job.

"Never mind," Alina said. "Let's split a beer at the terrace."

After Andrea picked up her racket they walked in silence. Alina was wounded as well. Although it was true she was not married, this condition was not the author of her dismay; it was her constant isolation. Returning home nightly at ten o'clock after a shattering day of work, and having only the creaking of her apartment floors greeting her was trying. She always switched on the television, but the banal shows didn't help. With her work hours, a social life was a formidable challenge. And even when she had the opportunity to meet people, meeting men who were truly secure enough not to be threatened by her abilities, who would not grow defensive and then belligerent at her possible future successes was a bleak prospect.

She anticipated their beer.

Wine swirled in his glass. John observed the gloomy whirlpool gradually cease rotating. Next he would try pouring at a different angle to see if the effect varied; a marvelously edifying activity. The wine was coolness on his lower lip, and he kept his lip submerged for several seconds before further tilting the glass and streaming the fluid across his tongue.

"Free markets are the secret," Cosmin pontificated.

John intermittently listened, even though Cosmin orated from high atop a stool in the center of John's living room. He had been lecturing sporadically for over an hour. Fortunately, or from John's perspective, lamentably, it was a stable piece of furniture, for Cosmin's massive wine intake had not steadied his balance.

Patrick sat silently in the corner, his lengthy fingers stroking the cotton fabric of his white shirt.

"Romania's recovery is based on the tenets of the investing world. Please remember gentlemen, before communism, this was one of the most beautiful countries in Europe," Cosmin announced. "Bucharest, in the south, was known as the Paris of the East before the communists leveled most of the buildings. All of our beautiful Cluj used to be lovely before they surrounded it with their buildings and factories."

John peered out the window. The sun had begun its descent, introducing warmer colors into the sky. Cosmin had stormed his apartment around three o'clock, bearing his usual spoils of wine, and when Patrick called an hour later John decided to allow him over. Perhaps he would dilute Cosmin's presence.

Surprisingly, the arrangement was relatively successful. All three imbibed for hours, and Cosmin, as usual, spoke about the various subjects he was studying on his path to his doctorate in political science. The degree had been, and would continue to be a lengthy road, John thought. Cosmin, in his mid-thirties, undoubtedly harbored massive deposits of knowledge on assorted subjects, and always ardently pursed fresh information, but he seemed oblivious as to how to weave all of this into a cohesive whole. The volume of Cosmin's voice was directly proportional to the amount of wine he absorbed, and after the disappearance of several bottles, his discourse could be heard at a fair distance.

Patrick's empty glass rested on the nearby table and his impassive gaze suggested he was registering little, if any, of Cosmin's oration. His suit jacket and white shirt, pressed when he had arrived, were now crumpled along with him in the depth of the chair. Animated an hour ago, he had informed John about a local clothing shop he discovered that sold a few Italian shirts, and he instantly purchased them all. One was even his size. But his disposition typically vacillated frequently and dramatically, and now he was mute.

The tall living room windows faced westward, with a clear view of the city and orange slashed sky. A cloud, high above, glided past with surprising pace.

"The painful recovery has just begun," Cosmin said.

It was time to be outside, John thought. He wanted to walk along Motilor Street and find a tiny side lane with a cafe. Venturing outside was a superb idea. He had spent this entire Sunday inside the apartment, the latter hours with these two delights. Of course Cosmin might become petulant if interrupted, though this wouldn't dissuade John, in fact it might serve as a bit of fuel for him to do so. And any interruption in his speech would only result in a transient trauma, as he would surely resume at a later venue precisely where he had left off.

"Time to go," John said.

Their steps lacked stability as they walked along Motilor Street. While toiling to maintain straight footfalls, Patrick bumped John and swerved away. Cosmin suggested various bars, pointing down each alley and enumerating the benefits of their respective drinking establishments. One would be prudent not to stake too much upon the verity of these lists. John declared they would continue to the park and to an outdoor terrace, whence they could watch the sky and people pass. The light was still strong enough and the chill wasn't overwhelming.

They found a small but crowded terrace café along the edge of the Parcul Central, and while Patrick departed for the bathroom to inspect the crispness of his collar, John seized the opportunity to order two bottles of local wine. The waiter nodded approvingly at John's order, which prompted him to suspect his choice of vintage. Patrick, perhaps on account of his smoothed shirt, returned reinvigorated. John inquired how his language lectures at the University were proceeding, but he dismissed the query with a terse "fine", and commented on the clothing choices of the patrons.

"People just never know what to wear."

"Do you?" John asked. Although Patrick undeniably dressed superbly, the smugness of his comment impelled John's need to rile him.

Patrick's cheeks colored and he turned to John. "Certainly."

John looked him up and down. "Then perhaps the day shalt arrive when thou shalt apply that knowledge?"

Patrick seized the trembling fingers of his left hand as he listed the establishments from where he had purchased each item of his clothing, but John interjected midway, laughing, and assured him that he was dressed splendidly. Patrick listened with damp eyes. He emptied his glass and, with a wrinkled brow, deliberated whether it was appropriate yet to move on after his chastisement; he didn't want to make things too easy. John, aware he hadn't entirely alleviated the suffering he evoked, decided further action was requisite.

"That scarf, where did you find it?"

Patrick gradually looked down at it. "Why?" he asked, stroking the fabric. "You feel the heathen need to insult it as well?"

John laughed. "Not at all. I have to admit it's wonderful."

The transformation was immediate. The rapidity with which he described the store in Bordeaux where he had discovered the scarf was amusing, and pauses to intake oxygen did not seem required. John smiled as Patrick continued about scarves he had considered but chose not to purchase. Some of them, he said, might have looked even finer than the one he currently wore, but he insisted that he wasn't ashamed of his decision. John refilled their glasses with the last of the wine and proposed a toast to Patrick's lost scarves. As their glasses clinked, and drops of the deep purple wine splashed onto their hands, Cosmin shoved John's shoulder.

"I know her," Cosmin said.

John looked around. "Whom?"

"She was a classmate of mine at University."

He was deliberately vague in an attempt to elicit questions, but he failed. Cosmin could not resist expounding on the subjects he raised, so a clear answer would come in time. At the tables surrounding them the plentiful clientele were casually dressed and conversed animatedly. The few fancier cafes and bars were in the Piata Unirii area, but John generally avoided those. And of course many bars throughout the city were underground caves, satiated with smoke and people who drank to forget; John certainly was not unfamiliar with these. This café, called Ziua, was a pleasant alternative, or at least it was so this evening.

Several feet away, two women approached an empty table, but another group, three men, arrived a second later. The middle-aged men all wore button down shirts and jackets, and hosted dark, full mustaches. The arrival times were proximate enough to leave the rightful claim upon the table in doubt. It was the sole empty table, and from the stolid expressions of the men and the firmness with which one gripped the chair, a display of chivalry did not appear forthcoming.

John watched amusedly as the taller of the women elegantly slid the gripped chair from the man's hands and motioned for her friend to sit. Her friend complied, and the taller woman, quite attractive, smiled briefly at the man and reclined on the chair beside her friend. They commenced conversing and ignored the men, who stared at them with calcified expressions of incredulity. Finding no alternative, they turned and walked away.

The women exchanged a laugh and the taller woman placed two tennis rackets on an empty chair beside her.

"I know her," Cosmin said, pushing John's shoulder once again. He stared at the women with the rackets.

"You seem proud of that fact."

Cosmin displayed what might have been a trace of vehemence, then grinned. "I knew her from back in school."

"Unless my mathematics are askew, two women are there."

"Actually, I went to school with both."

Patrick stared at the crowd in the opposite direction, disinterested in the current topic. John sensed Cosmin's desire to reveal more about the women, or woman, and he was startled that for once he actually wanted to hear more from him.

"Are you friends?" John asked.

Cosmin looked at John, the women, and at his empty glass. John motioned for a waiter and ordered another bottle of wine.

"I tried to be, but she is a bit difficult," Cosmin said.

"She?"

"The taller woman," he said. "The very pretty one."

"She is endowed with a name?"

"Alina. The other woman is Andrea."

The waiter arrived with the wine and opened the bottle. Patrick seized it and began pouring. John had to be sure to pay him some attention, lest he become overly irritable, and thus inquired whether he planned to visit his family's estate in France during the winter holiday. He assuredly did not, as there was absolutely no need to surround himself with that obsessively conservative environment. He might visit Thailand or Vietnam for a few weeks instead; he mentioned he could already speak a fair amount of Vietnamese. This was not surprising, for Patrick mastered languages with remarkable ease. Would John like to accompany him? John thanked him but said no, he didn't want to go anywhere.

"She might know more about business and finance than you," Cosmin said.

"Who?" John asked.

"Alina."

John sipped his wine. "The only subjects I know about these days are the local vintages," he said raising his glass, "and this is a fine one."

Cosmin laughed, stating that Alina was the dominant student in every year of college they attended together. She went on to graduate at the top of her class, and now was working for an investment company.

"So she hasn't done badly."

"She has," Cosmin said.

"You said found work in an investment company. That doesn't sound like a disaster."

Cosmin placed his wine glass onto the table and shifted closer to John. "For most it's not," he said in a hushed tone. "But for her, she should already be at least the head director. At least. Believe me, I went through a class with her. She embarrassed all of us."

"I believe any story where someone embarasses you," John said. "So what size company?"

Cosmin smiled. "Fairly small. But I know she really desires a job as a director."

"You're extolling her amazing abilities," John said. "So what's the problem?"

Cosmin's hand rested on John's shoulder. "Romania."

"What the hell does that mean?"

Cosmin laughed. "I hate to admit, and of course no one likes to believe this, but all recovery and change is slow. At least outside of your American movies."

Alina and Andrea were sipping beer.

"So it's hard for everyone," John said.

"Yes. And it doesn't help being a female."

"Is that so."

"Let's just say most of this part of the world still strongly believes she should do what women did and still primarily do: be a married mother at home with kids, and perhaps work a menial job," Cosmin said. "And her situation threatens all of them."

Sounds of clinking glasses filled the air. It was nearly dark outside, and many had transferred to the inside tables. The drinks were sinking in, and John noticed his left sleeve was darkly stained with wine. Patrick departed for the lavatory, and when John turned to Cosmin, the two women stood beside him.

"Alina, Andrea, this is John," Cosmin said, his face aglow.

John softly said hello. Alina stared at him with what John believed was an element of amusement.

"Alina, he might be the only person who is sharper than you," Cosmin said, laughing and proudly patting John. "He used to dominate the New York stock world. So beware. "

Alina inspected John up and down. A slight smile crept onto her face. John was instantly aware that his besmirched sweater and the bulwark of empty wine bottles before him did not create the most venerable presentation.

"He doesn't seem to be dominating much," Alina said.

Cosmin tapped the table with his fingers, looking apprehensively at John.

"That is simply not true," John announced. Everyone waited in silence for him to continue. "I want you to know that I did dominate, and to suggest otherwise is quite hurtful, actually," he said with his finger aloft. "I dominated today's drinking, gulping down far more fermented grape juice than both of my exceedingly accomplished fellow imbibers, and that, mind you, was no easy task."

He refilled his glass, the splashing wine the sole sound from their table. Cosmin laughed uneasily, his eyes darting from person to person, and he hurriedly raised the topic of old colleagues to Alina and Andrea. Both women, while speaking with Cosmin, peeked at John. After exchanging pleasantries, they departed. Alina nodded to John as she walked away.

# Chapter 8

The Romanian National Theater and Opera House was quite close to John's apartment. On the eastern end of Iuliu Maniu was the Piata Avram Iancu where the towering Orthodox Cathedral stood, and facing this piata, across Bulevardul Eroilor, was the Opera House. Built in 1906 by the Viennese theatre architects Fellner and Helmer, it's yellow façade seemed incongruous with the darker buildings in the vicinity.

John had passed this building numerous times during his first months, but had never taken the time to carefully observe it. Two weeks ago, it had been drizzling continuously on a Saturday morning, and the sky revealed no intention of clearing. John walked down his street without a destination in mind and didn't notice his sweater dampening after a few minutes in the rain. He had spent his entire morning reading a collection of regional short stories. Crossing into the Piata Avram Iancu he paused, wiping the rainwater from his brow. Before him, across the street, was the Opera House. Something piqued his interest, and as he stared he realized he was drawn to the building's solitude from its surroundings. It was blockaded by streets on three sides, with a small park in the back. No one entered or left, or even milled in its vicinity. The entire scene was acutely sedate. He chose to cross over to the entrance and induce, from proximate observation, if the theater was indeed functioning.

A cobblestone drive curved to the front doors. Tall and painted white with frosted glass, they were shut and locked, and through the glass he observed only darkness. He looked to both sides, expecting someone to appear, perhaps demanding to know what his business was, but there was only the rain. Moving to explore the theater's sides, he noticed a bleached poster for Cavalleria Rusticana that stated the show was supposedly commencing in two weeks, on a Friday, Saturday, and Sunday. But where was the box office? As he looked up at the building he noticed the condition of the paint: it was peeling, and not solely in single spot, but throughout. Years had transpired since the last coat. Along the theater's massive side, he encountered nothing but two sealed doors. The tiny park in the rear comprised a cement plaza with benches and a few dark pines. The lone person present was a withered man wearing a grey cap, seated on a bench and oblivious to the precipitation. He would not strike one as being a stronghold of reliable information, but due to a lack of options, John asked where the theater sold tickets. He peered at John vacantly, his eyes a single milky hue, and then grinned, seemingly amused. John repeated his inquiry, and the man raised his arm, coated with the worn tweed sleeve of an oversized suit jacket, and pointed across the street where lay a few bars and a store. He congealed in this pointed position, and John, after a moment dedicated to gripping his chin while staring at the man in befuddlement, at least realized movement was not imminent, and hence proceeded in the suggested direction.

Across the street were two tiny bars encased in clouds of smoke. A narrow cigarette store followed that could perchance fit

two gaunt people inside. Beyond was the street corner. No box office was here. What did catch his attention, on the decrepit door
to his left, was a scratched plastic window fastened to its upper
half. A barely legible handwritten sign was taped obliquely to this
plastic, and after closer analysis he deciphered that it stated opera
tickets were for sale. No one seemed to be stationed at this window,
but at its base he spotted a blue bandana, and correctly surmised
it was the adornment atop of someone's head. This seated person
apparently was not overextending herself in an attempt to peddle
tickets. John stood beside the window and the bandana remained
static, so he bumped his hand against the plastic. The plump,
weathered face of an aged woman looked up, her eyes squinting in
bewilderment, and after several moments of her gauging her surroundings, she demanded to know, in the form of multiple grunts,
what he wanted. He informed her of his interest in opera tickets.
This took several moments to register. She finally reached to the
ground and handed him a crumpled seating chart with ticket prices besieged by murky stains. To the stupefaction of the woman, he
purchased a single orchestra level ticket, near the stage, for each
of the first three nights.

John arrived fifteen minutes before the show's commencement. He was relieved to see, as he approached from the distance,
at least light emanating from the theater. That was a start. Several
cars were parked in the curved drive. John wore a scarf and blazer,
and he had partaken of a bottle of local merlot before arriving.
An elderly man with an extraordinarily protracted nose and wearing a tuxedo a few sizes too large collected his ticket at the front
entrance. John entered the grand lobby, adorned with red carpets
and a wide, curved limestone staircase in the center that sent

tributaries rising to both sides of the room. The ceiling was high enough that he could barely discern the paintings of figures on its marble surface, and a chandelier hung by a copper chain over the room's center. Few people walked about. His black shoes contrasted sharply with the red carpet that was, in certain spots, worn entirely through to the chalk-colored floor. A corpulent, bearded man pulling on a cigar and wearing a starched tuxedo stood by the doors to the orchestra. He stared intensely at John, and John glanced over his shoulder to see if someone behind him was the true recipient of this severe glare. No one else was there.

John entered the orchestra and pondered his longstanding fascination with theaters. He enjoyed theatrical performances, but also possessed a fondness for the buildings themselves. The anticipation and tension that thrived continuously within them during rehearsals and shows, and even when empty, enticed him. An empty theater, with lights extinguished, whispered from numerous places and the performances past echoed from the stage. Sadly but predictably, John in his past had rarely taken time away from his work to attend the theaters he so appreciated.

The orchestra level was lined with rows of red padded seats, and ornately carved balconies overlooked the room from the sides. By now, the lack of maintenance was clearer, as he observed the chips on the balcony facades and the insipid paint coating the walls. Still, the lure wasn't entirely gone; he sensed that this was once, perhaps a long time ago, an august, pulsing theater. Filaments of that charm lingered.

A grand total of three people stood at the edge of the mezzanine, all observing the activity below. Although the show would start in ten minutes, the orchestra seating area wasn't even a quarter filled. This was particularly perturbing as this was the production's premier. He found himself suddenly concerned for the performers, for like all performers they yearned for an audience.

But what prompted his emotion? After months under the influence of fermented grapes and wallowing solely in his personal sorrows, these were unfamiliar feelings. He moved down the center aisle towards the stage and located his seat a few rows from the orchestra pit. As he sat alone and studied his single-page program, several of the violinists observed him with curiosity and conferred. The mostly barren rows behind him contained a few elderly couples. His row, two from the pit, was bare except for a couple at the opposite end. Moments before the lights dimmed, he turned and checked the room, hoping for at least a slight augmentation in audience size, but attendance hadn't altered. He could not be sure, but the couples sitting in the distance seemed to observe and discuss him. But he was not sure.

He placed his program on the seat beside him and realized its base was not fastened properly; the left side angled towards the floor. The lights dimmed and the orchestra commenced.

The show was not spectacular. Although the sets were minimal, quality performances could always ameliorate the production. Yet most of the actors, with a few exceptions, did not seem overly inspired. To a degree this was understandable. John still found enjoyment in the bits of enthusiasm that surfaced. After the final act the meager audience applauded diffidently. John watched the actors and orchestra passively absorb this listless response, their lifeless faces staring blankly ahead, and he found himself standing and clapping. The performers turned to him, stunned, but no one else in the audience followed his lead, and their eyes singed his back. There was no curtain call.

He attended performances on the next two evenings, and applauded ardently after each one. The cast had begun to look towards him at the end of the shows, and he made a note to purchase tickets for future performances.

It was warm for the middle of November. John would be attending a Friday evening performance of La Traviata. The theater was familiar to him, as he had consistently attended shows for nearly a month. That afternoon he had ignored calls from Cosmin, but later that night he indubitably would hear from him again. John relieved a bottle of wine of the burden of its contents before strolling the short distance to the theater.

The audience was even sparser than the usual lean crowd: at most twenty people with perhaps a few more on the mezzanine. John took his regular seat two rows from the orchestra. He now knew each of the orchestra members and actors by face. Two violin players, a man and woman with auburn hair and green eyes who were twins, waved enthusiastically at him with their bows as was now their custom. The orchestra members, a talented group, represented a wide spectrum of ages. A few members appeared to be in their sixties, while one cellist was in her late teens. At times they lacked inspiration, but at certain moments, when absorbed in their craft, the sounds floated through the theater, and John passed into another realm. As for the actors, he curiously observed the same ones perform on different nights; it was the national opera, so the same actors were employed by the theater for the various shows. Their appearances and body motions were now familiar, but beyond that, he began to perceive personalities. One fine actress, listed as Lavinia on the programs, who played leading female roles and normally wore a grave countenance, had laughed momentarily a few times while exchanging somber lines. In fairness, the chuckling was subtle, and the audience was unlikely to have noticed. Yet these inconspicuous expulsions of laughter troubled John, not for the minor break in the performance, but rather they seemed a release, a discharge of some uneasiness or frustration that lurked about. Something was amiss.

When applause came, the actors now unabashedly looked towards John with diversified smiles. Whether they found it absurd that he attended shows constantly and alone, or were flattered by his presence, or perhaps both, they undoubtedly derived enjoyment from him.

The first scenes of La Traviata flowed smoothly. John was pleased that finally, the icebergs in the audience followed his lead and actually clapped with some conviction. As John stood for intermission, a young boy wearing a tiny maroon vest and white shirt approached, handed him an envelope and dashed away.

"Visit us backstage after show—the cast." John instinctively peered at the stage, but was greeted only by the closed curtains.

During the final act, admittedly a bit distracted, he watched the actors with heightened scrutiny, wondering who had actually written the note. It was signed "the cast", so it had the appearance of a group effort. They certainly had discussed him. Yes, he must be a peculiar sight sitting there alone. By now they surely knew by rumor or by his slightly different dress that he was a foreigner. At least the impression he made must have been somewhat positive, for chances are they did not invite him for a backstage flogging.

During the curtain call it seemed all the actors stared at him with amplified intensity. After they disappeared behind the curtain, he was unsure of how to proceed. He was tempted to just depart and return to his apartment. That was his usual move. But they awaited him backstage, even though they had failed to include the minor detail of how to get there. He expected one of the actors to emerge and guide him, but the stage was silent. What did they want him backstage for anyway? The audience had dispersed.

He considered leaving for his apartment once again, for in his pantry were wine bottles that he had indecorously ignored for almost a day, and he turned to depart and redress this crass behavior.

He then noticed a small door beside the orchestra pit that he had spotted several weeks ago, and chose to quickly peek inside. He entered a dim, curving hallway with peeling algae-colored wallpaper. A robust mildew odor replaced the slightly musty air of the theater. At the end of the hall was sallow light. He was drawn forward, pursuing this light, and emerged into a tiny room with a worn wooden floor and a table covered by dark wigs. No one was present. Voices escaped from beyond another door ahead. He paused before it and listened. It was amusing that he hesitated to open the door; he felt like a schoolboy. Finally he opened it, at least partially, revealing a spacious dressing room with the cast sitting by mirrors and scrubbing off their makeup, chatting, and jostling about. He peered through the half-opened door. Fortunately, a lanky man who played minor roles spotted him and yelled something terse but incomprehensible, and within seconds everyone summoned him inside and merged around him.

"Finally you're here," a woman said, standing beside the doorway. She was tall and sturdily built, and John recognized her from her various character roles. She forcefully tugged him by his wrist deeper into the room, and the group followed. For the next minutes John shook hands and answered questions concerning where he was from, from where his love of the opera originated, and what he thought of their shows compared to those he had seen in other countries. In truth he had only experienced an opera every few years, and only here in Cluj did he start attending constantly, but no need to mention this. He praised their shows, that he did, but not unduly, for their work simply did not merit such exaltation due to the general malaise of the performers. And the actors, although they would be flattered by lofty compliments, would surreptitiously wonder if he was being veracious, or perhaps lacked knowledge about the subject matter. Yet he stayed positive, for he had detected slight improvements and some effort was exerted into the performances. He stated he was fortunate to be residing nearby, with the chance to watch them often.

Lavinia's attractive face was recognizable even though it was partially covered with cream; she stared at him from across the room. As the group's attention finally subsided and he was able to address individuals, he approached her. When he neared she quickly leaned against the wall in an attempt to evince a nonchalant demeanor, but suddenly found the angle far more radical than expected, and she struggled mightily to mind her position without revealing any effort. John was heedful not to expose his awareness of her exertion.

"I enjoyed the performance."

"Did you really?" she responded with an insouciant air.

"Certainly."

She swept her arm across the room. "They are all happy to see you."

"Does 'they' include you?"

Lavinia's lips rose slightly. "I must ask why you attend our shows so often."

"Is it a problem?"

"No, not at all," she promptly said, straightening herself with a slight stumble. "It's no problem, of course not."

"I enjoy being inside the theater."

Lavinia checked the room to see if anyone listened to her. "My performances," she said in a softer tone, "have you enjoyed them?"

"You are asking about all of them, or a particular one?"

She heartily laughed, her lengthy hair sliding over her shoulders. After exhaling, she looked around the room again. "I do what I can here."

"Of course."

Alina now stared at the floor, in what appeared to be a morose manner.

"You're doing a good job; you're a very good leading lady," John said.

"But they offer us very little."

"Meaning?"

She started moving towards an empty corner of the room without saying anything, and John, checking the milling actors across the room, followed. "He deprives us of most of our pay," she said in a hushed tone. "The city and state subsidize the theater, but we barely get anything. And our production needs, he ignores them entirely. It's no wonder we aren't taken seriously by anyone." Her eyes were moist.

"I'm sorry to hear that." John was unsure of whom she referred to, and was startled by the dour turn their conversation had taken.

"If we complain, or say anything, we are gone."

"I see."

"I don't mean to complain to you."

"You're not complaining, you're just telling me what it's like. So who is this 'he' you're mentioning?"

She turned away. "I don't want to discuss all that."

"I understand," John said. "So you mentioned it's difficult."

She looked directly at John. "Do you really want to know?" She spoke in a whisper. "We work full time here, and I still have to live in a small apartment with my parents, sleeping on a couch. I have no choice. None of us do."

Water welled in her eyes. He was surprised by and tried to quell the sympathy that was flooding inside of him.

"Well that's absurd, considering the wonderful performances you give," John said. She stared down at her pale hands that she kneaded by her waist. Several actors beckoned John from across the room.

"I really should go," he said.

"We'll see you soon?"

"Of course you will." He walked away and wanted to leave the room, but more cast members approached him. He kept the exchanges centered on their performances and away from himself. This was not difficult. Although they were curious about him, they were actors, and ultimately desired to ascertain his opinion on their performances. And though they enthusiastically discussed the opera with him, he began to detect, as they grew more comfortable with his presence, a hanging fog of melancholy amongst all of them. This further distressed him, and his longstanding instinct was to distance himself from this pain. He excused himself by announcing that he eagerly anticipated tomorrow's show, and departed swiftly through the dank hallway.

Outside the theater the air struck him crisply. The weather had cooled significantly since he entered, and it was dark. He surveyed the scenery from the front doors. Streetlights illuminated concentrated sections of the Piata Avram Iancu across the street.

"So you went backstage?"

The voice startled him. A woman stood by the doorway, to his right, with a program in her hands. The lights from the theater were strong enough that he could see her features. She was familiar; he recognized her from their brief meeting while he had sat with Cosmin at a café by the park. She had been with a friend.

"Alina, correct?"

She nodded.

"No tennis racket?" She didn't respond. Was she outside here waiting for him? "And how did you know I was backstage?"

"By observing." Her expression revealed as little as her answer.

"And the opera, did you enjoy it?"

"Even with the lack of sets or costumes, yes," she said. "They still manage to put on a decent show."

The wind arose and Alina adjusted her jacket.

"Where did you sit?" he said.

Alina stepped onto the cobblestones of the curved drive, and suggested he join her. "Up in the mezzanine, where I always sit."

As they slowly walked, John turned to her. She wore a navy business suit under an open black coat, and her hair was tied tightly back. "You attend often?" he asked.

"Perhaps not as often as you," she said laughing. "Work won't allow it. But once a month if I can, maybe twice."

John smiled. "So you've seen me here."

"It's difficult not to notice you with only fifteen others in the audience and you always in that same seat up front. And you're the only one who attends alone."

"Besides you that is."

"Oh?" she said, her eyebrows aloft. "Maybe I'm here with a different person each time."

"Well, all those different people must be on vacation tonight," John said, inducing her laughter.

They crossed the street into the piata, and continued onto Iuliu Maniu.

"Still playing any tennis?" John said.

"I try, but the weather is becoming a problem."

Looking at Alina was intoxicating. Her hair was the color of the night. Light was not in grand supply on his street, but her large aquamarine eyes, focused on him, were sharply visible. She observed things intensely. Those eyes penetrated, revealing her intelligence; they must intimidate many.

"So," he asked, after halting. "Outside the theater. Were you standing there waiting for me?" The question was candid and direct, and he expected her to flinch. At least that was his intention. She did not.

"Yes."

Now he began to hesitate. "Why?"

"Why did you leave New York?"

"What?"

"New York. Why did you leave?" Her tone contained a trace of sympathy.

Her question surprised him. And disturbed him. Why ask him about his reasons for leaving? "I wanted to go on an extended wine tasting tour," he said. "I've been successful with the wine tasting, but lately the touring element has been lacking."

She smiled slightly and pressed on; wry comments did not dissuade her.

"Before Romania, where did you go?"

"Plenty of countries across Europe. I started in Portugal and traveled east."

"And why leave your great life in the Manhattan markets?"

John crushed a cobalt can under his foot. "I assume you're getting your data from Cosmin. Might I mention that he's not always a bastion of reliable information."

The streetlight directly above them flickered and buzzed severely, creating alternating images of her face, with what appeared to be the discordant emotions of fascination in the light and frustration in the dimness.

"I've known him long enough to detect his truths from his hyperboles."

"Perhaps," John said. "But maybe he doesn't possess your exquisite talent. Maybe I've fed him inaccurate information."

This comment affected Alina, for she took time to consider it. "I doubt it. He said it took him months to get just that little bit of data."

John began to walk again, involuntarily kicking tiny rocks that clacked against the larger cobblestones, but he could not feel them through his hard-soled shoes. He noted that a well-placed slap atop Cosmin's head would be beneficial for all. Alina glided noiselessly.

"Well I'm flattered that you're curious," he said.

Alina walked in front of him. "You never answered my question."

"That doesn't change the fact that I'm flattered." John halted in front of his building. "I live here. But let me guess, you already know that."

"You live here? Is at least that accurate information?" she said, smiling.

"I really do hope so, because I intend to sleep inside there."

Alina peered up at the cloudless sky; the stars were sharply visible across the dark panorama. "Maybe I shall see you at the opera sometime," she said.

"You know how it works. I will be the odd sort alone up front," John said, and he turned and entered his building. Inside was cold. The thick stone walls magnanimously spread the chill. Quite an audacious woman, John thought. Absurd, in fact. Thank heavens I'm alone again. But after ascending to the top floor and before pouring his first glass of wine, he was startled to find himself looking out his bedroom window and scanning the street below for a glimpse of Alina. He saw only the aged Dacia automobiles parked along the sidewalk. The lone sound was the snapping and buzzing of the streetlamp.

# Chapter 9

When Cosmin telephoned later that night, John answered. While this was assuredly an atypical response, he felt compelled to speak with anyone, even Cosmin. Cosmin's hello was muffled by voices and striking glasses.

"My friend...my good friend," Cosmin said. The demonstrative display and slight slurring revealed that his drinking had commenced at least several hours previous.

"What charming location are you planted in now?" John said.

"At a place that lacks the fine drink stock of your apartment. But I shall stop by soon, and I will bring both a fine bottle and good conversation."

"Considering I've never known you to provide either," John said, "I won't delude myself into believing you're bringing both. Either way, there'll be no need."

Cosmin laughed. "Why my friend, do you have ample stock?"

"I'll meet you there."

"What? Out here?" Cosmin paused, gauging whether John's comment was facetious. "I'm shocked; you actually meeting me out to socialize, and before our drinking commenced at your abode! But no need to joke with me. Just remain and I'll be there in ten minutes."

"Where are you?"

"You are humorous tonight."

"Where are you?"

Cosmin hesitated. "At Vulpe."

"I'll see you there."

The air was burdened by viscous moisture. Vulpe was an underground cave bar with limited lighting, surprisingly crowded. Cosmin was not immediately apparent. The music emerging from the bare sound system was more of a vague fuzzy reverberation than anything appreciable. All the rusted tables were occupied. The odor of cigarette smoke was intense enough that after several inhalations John no longer smelled it. Although a bar was to the side, and people clustered against the walls and in the murky corners, Cosmin usually preferred a table to serve as a base for his lectures.

There he was, at a table along the far wall with a woman and two men. So at least there would be others to converse with. When his eyes met John's from halfway across the room he summarily, with short words and a dismissive motion, cleared the table.

John sat on a teetering chair. "What happened to everyone sitting here with you?"

Cosmin donned a confounded expression. "Who?"

"The three people you instructed to leave five seconds ago."

"Ahh," Cosmin said, looking away. "They wanted to chat with others."

"Really? Quite a rapid and simultaneous decision they all made."

Cosmin still looked aside.

"You know, we can speak and socialize with others," John

said. "It doesn't have to be just you and me."

"Of course."

"It doesn't always have to be Cosmin speaking with John."

"Of course not."

John knew he must pursue this avenue. It disturbed Cosmin, but it had to be explored. John needed to begin to meet with others, but Cosmin relished being his sole focus and John, for his part, had never demanded otherwise. Now when John wasn't present, mind you, Cosmin was quite a popular individual and had a multitude of people he socialized with.

"So you said. But when you dismissed everyone at this table as I approached, were you worried about them, or about me?"

"Not at all my friend…"

"Or perhaps," John interjected, "you're worried about my impression of you when you interact with others?"

Cosmin exhaled. "Yes of course we should talk to many people. Of course. How else can we comprehend the intricacies and dynamics of both society and life?"

"Or have a conversation."

It was past twelve and the bar remained densely crowded. John scanned the tables around them.

"Different from the bars at home I'm sure," Cosmin said. He wanted to hear about John's past, but knew of John's aversion to speaking about it, and was thus attempting to be clever.

John refilled his glass with the last of the inky wine. He continued to tilt the bottle, letting a few final drops reunite with their compatriots.

"But I guess they have everything there in New York," Cosmin tried.

John stroked the curdled smoke before him with a gentle brush of his left hand, believing he could feel the texture of the grayish cloud.

"So do you ever miss it?" Cosmin finally bluntly asked. His venture into ingenuity had been a stunted and feckless journey. He recoiled when John turned towards him.

Cosmin's tension offered some amusement. John would spare him any vitriol. "Sometimes," John said, "when I'm in a crowded place like this, and I'm not listening to anything specific but just the general din, sometimes then it seems, if for a moment, that I'm back."

Cosmin was transfixed; he stared ahead, seemingly lost. Finally he softly spoke: "You would like to be back?"

"What would I like? Perhaps I would like if you would bring one of your friends back to the table with you."

After hesitating, clearly disappointed with the answer, Cosmin arose. He did not return for ten minutes, and upon doing so, a short man, about Cosmin's age and with closely trimmed hair, stood obediently by his side. Cosmin introduced him and placed a bottle in the center of the table.

"Hello Florin," John said.

Florin curtly nodded without orally responding; his trepidation evidenced that he had endured a thorough rehearsal for this meeting. Drinks were poured and Cosmin began praising John's abilities. Florin listened without much movement, although it should be mentioned that he did blink twice. He still had not spoken.

It was time to modify the dynamics at the table. "Don't listen to what Cosmin is saying," John said. "Not only do I advise that in this specific case, but as a general rule."

Florin, constraining a smile, checked both of them, weighing whether laughing was prudent. When Cosmin finally chuckled, Florin emancipated his emotion with brief laughter.

Seeing Florin relax, at least slightly, pleased John. "And yes, I was well-known within certain circles for my buying and selling securities in New York," John said, "but who cares anyway? Don't

THE SUNLIGHT LIES BEYOND

let him go on with this nonsense as if I'm some sort of quality person or hero. Believe me Florin, I'm the furthest thing from that. I've always been self-centered and pathetic."

"Don't be ridiculous, my friend," Cosmin quickly said, as his eyes darted apprehensively from John to Florin. John's comments had disconcerted him. "Why are you talking like this? You were known as the best, and you've helped many others with your work."

John laughed heartily. *"Others?"*

His sardonic tone alarmed Cosmin, who once again checked Florin. "Yes, your brilliant work helped the wonderful American economy and has helped many," he said, a slight quiver to his voice.

*"Many?"* John said, continuing to laugh.

Cosmin glanced at Florin.

John pushed his glass forward, scraping the reddish metal of the table. "I tried to help myself; that's it. That's who I wanted to help. At least get that straight. Now if your definition of many is 'John', so be it," he said. Cosmin listened, unnerved, while Florin was fascinated. "I toiled from the very start to see how far I could help myself. That was the mission," He pressed his forefinger against the maroon dust. "And ultimately I didn't even do a great job with that, now did I?" he said, exhibiting his dust-covered fingertip to both of them.

Cosmin retorted rapidly. "Don't be absurd my friend. You earned great money, you represented capitalism, and that is what is desperately needed here." He turned to Florin, emitting an artificial laugh. "We've all had a lot to drink tonight."

"What is needed here or not needed here is a separate issue," John said. "But what I represented was myself and myself alone." John paused, rubbing his palms together. "And in reference to drink, we are in agreement there: we've all had our share, but that is not noteworthy news."

Florin had been silent the entire time.

"Are you working these days, Florin?" John asked.

"Actually, I am," he said, straightening himself in his chair, clearly pleased that John had addressed him.

The table jarred, and the woman who had struck it backed away, apologizing to John. She stumbled against another woman and they both chortled.

"So what type of work are you doing?" John asked as he righted the glasses.

"Actually, I'm working as a sales agent at a new travel agency."

Cosmin observed John and Florin, turning from head to head as they spoke, and then began to say: " What Florin is saying…"

"I believe Florin displayed that his vocal cords are fully operational," John said. He turned back to Florin. "What I'm curious about, Florin, is how is the travel business? Or to phrase it another way, are many people here traveling?"

Florin leaned forward, sampled his wine for the first time, and spoke with a firmer timbre. "Actually, it's slow. Money is still not plentiful." Cosmin remained mute, a monumental struggle for him, while Florin drank more, invigorated by his receptive audience. "But more important is the mindset," he continued, "because after over forty years of communism, when travel was barely permitted, the people have still not developed the mentality that travel, especially for pleasure, is an option. To them it still seems a violation." He imperceptibly raised his chin, contented with his answer.

"A violation?" John said. "A violation of what?"

Florin shook his head. "Of that I am unsure."

His transformation from timidity to assurance pleased John. He seemed a levelheaded and bright man. "So Florin, what do you see happening?"

"Of that I am unsure. No one truly knows what is happening in Romania now. Everything is a mystery."

"And change, Florin, do you see it coming?"

"It will take some time to change," he said, looking directly at John. "I just pray it will."

John fastened the top button of his coat. The winds in late November arose suddenly and harshly. He didn't abhor inclement weather; rather he often enjoyed it. When vigorous, cold winds blew, or heavy rains or sleet fell, pedestrians on the streets tended to move swiftly minding themselves, and John could stroll without being disturbed and observe those around him without being noticed.

The Manastur district comprised mostly tall apartment buildings. Located on the western portion of the city, the buildings, constructed after the Second World War, were erected hastily without regard for their visual impact. John walked down Calea Floresti, and these sour structures loomed on both sides, forming a canyon that enabled the wind to gain momentum. He dipped his chin into his jacket for respite.

During warmer weather, many people in this neighborhood, lacking extensive agendas, lingered in the building entrances or in groups along the sidewalk. Now only a few people could be seen.

The interstices between the heavy gray clouds permitted only strands of light to filter through. John moved eastward, back towards the city center. Passing an apartment structure, he noticed a woman with a raised jacket collar and a woolen hat lowered to just above her eyes glance at him twice while approaching the building's entrance. Her staccato movement piqued his curiosity. As he neared, and between the vertical walls of her coat collar, he recognized Alina.

"What are you doing out here?" she said, upon sighting him. She appeared unnerved.

"Have I ever complimented you on your quaint greeting skills?"

She turned away, facing the building entrance.

"You live here?" John asked.

"My grandmother does," Alina said, pulling at her already raised collar. "It's cold; I'm going inside."

Her curtness was surprising. His presence did not seem to please her, which was unexpected, as the previous time they had met outside the Opera House she had pursued him. He could be assertive with her as well.

"I'll join you on your visit to grandmother."

"No, that's fine."

"Oh it's absolutely no trouble. Since I sense you're overjoyed at seeing me here, I'll indulge you by joining you."

Alina shook her head. "We'll talk another time."

"Yes we will," John said. "And we'll also talk this time, at your grandmother's." He glanced at the ominous gray wall before them. "So shall we enter? As you mentioned, it's cold."

"We'll meet another time John," she said, passing through the doorway.

He squinted amidst the wind gusts, unsure how to proceed. Her departure had been efficient. One thing was clear; she didn't want him at this location. Perhaps this grandmother was unwell. Only one option existed. He entered the building and listened for her footfalls on the stairs. She still climbed, already several stories above. He ascended noiselessly, two stairs per step. On the fifth floor, she exited the staircase. John entered that hallway, a bland cement tunnel, and listened. An elderly woman's barking rattled from midway, and standing beside the door, he could hear Alina's terse responses.

The interaction bothered him. It was not entirely audible, but it was clear the snapping voice was chiding and disparaging Alina.

He experienced a twinge of anger. His knock on the door surprised him, and apparently those inside, for it elicited silence.

A withered physiognomy emerged and demanded to know his purpose. He mentioned he was a friend of Alina's and had come to say hello to both of them. A thin grin spread across her face, and she invited John inside with effusive body language unanticipated from someone her age, or of any age. Alina stood across the room and said nothing, but from her steadfast posture and glare, John surmised she would be quite contented to hurl him out the kitchen window.

"Alina, do you want to introduce me to your handsome friend?" her grandmother said in a sugary but admonishing tone.

After a brief introduction, he shook grandmother's hand and said he was pleased to meet her. She insisted John remain for food, but John said: "Well I must first of course ask Alina how she would feel."

"Delighted," Alina responded, and John admired the adeptness with which she cloaked her desire to see him airborne.

The small apartment's walls had been white some time long ago, and the plastic tabletop beside the half kitchen was grooved from use. They encircled this table with bowls of soup before them.

"How long have you known my granddaughter?"

"For some time now."

Grandmother stirred Alina's soup. "It's good to see you," she said. "You see, Alina doesn't have many friends, especially male."

Alina consumed her soup with her head near to the bowl.

"Considering her beauty, I'm surprised to hear that," John said. Alina's corner of her mouth arose slightly, and grandmother retorted viciously.

"Attractiveness means nothing if unused," she said. "Then it's wasted."

"Some don't need to use it," Alina said.

"Eat that soup."

"Some can actually rely on their abilities," she said.

"Alone," she said, pointing her wet spoon at Alina. Cloudy droplets precipitated onto the table. "You're always alone, so eat that soup."

They all returned to the consumption of the soup, a foggy liquid with carrot and potato and strands of dusky chicken. John prodded a vegetable slice, which at first he believed was a potato, but was a carrot drained of color.

"Alina's mother was married at twenty," grandmother said, "and Alina is now thirty-seven."

John and Alina stirred their soup.

"I was married at eighteen," she said. "Alina is thirty-seven."

"I understand Alina was the finest student in her University," John said, placing his nicked silver spoon onto the plate. "And now she's an assistant director at a company."

Were those actual flames in grandmother's eyes? "Work is work," she said, "but a husband and family are the most important and my Alina can't do that."

"Certainly Alina is capable of anything she wants."

Grandmother scoffed. "Do you like good cooking?" she asked him, motioning to the soup. John did, and felt the urge to mention he looked forward to encountering some, but he restrained himself and stated the soup was fine.

"Even Alina might learn to cook," grandmother said.

"Actually I had one of her soups; it was excellent, superb," he said, unsure if Alina had ever prepared a soup or even a sandwich.

Alina glanced at him and grandmother dropped her spoon onto the table; it clanged loudly.

"And a great-grandchild, that would be nice," she said, staring at Alina.

"Wouldn't it?" Alina said.

"Don't get clever," grandmother said, gaining momentum. "She's alone all the time. I don't have a great-grandchild, and she doesn't even visit me. Her work obsession is just foolishness; it's selfishness." She grabbed a ladle and doled more soup into their bowls. "Selfishness."

After the soup was finished, John announced his departure.

Grandmother gripped his arm with surprising strength as she guided him and cordially told him it was her pleasure to have such a handsome man visit, and he should return any time. She asked, while coyly smiling and exhibiting false teeth, to please forgive her Alina for such rude conduct. John halted, and composedly informed her that Alina, as usual, had only been lovely. She stared at him befuddled, maintaining her clutch on his arm, uncertain how to deal with him; apparently he was something new she had never encountered. She ushered him out the door.

The wind hadn't ceased. John stood on the sidewalk alongside the building's entrance. As dusk deepened, tiny lights began to flicker on in windows across the street. He considered moving, but remained, hoping Alina would come down.

Alina soon emerged. "So did you enjoy her display?" she said. She wasn't wearing her coat or hat, and her hair was at the wind's mercy.

"Did you actually ever make a soup?" John said.

Alina's hands glided across her face, attempting to clear the fluttering hair. "I'm glad you were amused by that."

"The soup?"

"Her behavior. It's nothing new."

John paused. "Why tolerate it?"

"Tolerate it?" Alina asked, stiffening.

"Yes, exactly."

Alina's laugh was hearty, but not without a tinge of derision. "And what would you have me do?"

"Perhaps a bit of a discussion."

Alina laughed again. "Your complete lack of understanding is amusing."

John was irked. "I am not claiming to have a complete comprehension of the situation. Far from that. But I'm aware when someone is being abused."

"There's nothing to do." Forcefully, she parted the hair draped over her face. "Her stubbornness is immoveable. I visit quickly, we argue a bit and I let her have her say, and I get out. Changing her is not possible."

"How often are you visiting?"

"Almost every week."

John paused. "But why so often?"

"Did I mention she's my grandmother?"

"I believe you did."

"And when I first moved to this city, and couldn't afford rent, I lived with her. Unpleasant for sure, but she did cook for me and I stayed for two years."

John considered those past years and how utterly unbearable each day must have been. How did she make it through? That was a feat worthy of reverence. "I understand. Her behavior just seems a bit extreme."

"What isn't extreme here?" Alina yelled. "What have you seen that isn't?"

The wind persisted. "Cosmin mentioned your job is fine."

"I believe we've covered the reliability of Cosmin," Alina said. "I run that entire company for all of them, and I'm only an assistant director; that's all. I barely receive any thanks. And promotions are always limited for someone like me."

John ruminated the "someone like me", and didn't like its flavor. Alina's skin had reddened from the elements and exasperation.

"And the *alone*. She never fails to mention I'm alone," Alina said.

"At least she's consistent," John said playfully, but received no reaction. "Let's not forget, I'm not sitting with an entourage at the opera either."

Humor didn't solace her. "Obviously being alone is not a major concern of yours, is it?" Alina said.

"Hopefully not, or I would be in considerable trouble."

Alina stared at him. "In truth, not much of anything seems to be a concern for you," she said. "Am I correct?"

Her words stung, and stung deeply. Perhaps in the past there had been some truth to them. Yet he wanted to tell her that much did concern him, he did care, but he had never discovered the way to act on these feelings. She observed him intently, desiring his response. "I would like to say this meeting has been absolutely delightful," John said. "But to avert the extremes we've mentioned, and to avoid prevarication, I will instead say it's been interesting." He gracefully bowed and walked away, refraining from looking back. And no, she didn't call to him. As he strode along the sidewalk, he noticed several streetlamps were blackness. Disquieting sounds, akin to moaning, emerged from buildings as the wind rushed through them.

# Chapter 10

John stared at the page but the words did not register. The second time he received a call he answered. Patrick's impassioned voice beseeched him to join him at Vista café, for extremely pressing business of course. Not wanting to stay alone, he capitulated to the requests. It was past ten o'clock. He had returned several hours ago from his rendezvous with Alina and her delightful grandmother, and since then he had only gazed at the ceiling and the same brittle page of a treatise on primary causes of the fall of the Western Roman Empire; quite a productive time.

Silence owned the streets, but when he arrived at Vista a fair amount of people sat inside. Patrick waived animatedly from a table near the rear.

"You came," Patrick said.

"You invited me here to make brilliant observations?"

Patrick poured John a glass of wine and raised his for a toast.

"So what is it?" John asked, his glass still on the table.

"Sadly, it's a local merlot. I sincerely apologize if the vintages dearer to my heart weren't available but ..."

"What have you asked me here for?"

Patrick resembled a nonplussed child.

"You demanded I come here. 'Urgent', you cried."

Patrick again raised his glass to no reciprocation.

"The reason?" John said firmly.

Patrick sighed. He spilled some wine onto the table and endeavored to mop it with his thumb and forefinger, and John realized he had underestimated the level of Patrick's inebriation.

"The need to profess my amorous feelings has finally arisen," Patrick announced, while surveying the establishment.

"I see." This could be trouble. He didn't want Patrick saying things he would lament the next day, and considering Patrick's drunken and mercurial state, this was a distinct possibility. John, immersed in the current dilemma, momentarily forgot his own tribulations.

"Regrettably, you're not the least bit interested. That has been obvious enough," Patrick said, looking away, "but perhaps he is." He pointed to a table in the corresponding corner, occupied by three men and a woman. "Maybe that tall gentleman."

John tasted his wine and impending trouble. "What has led you to suspect this alleged interest of his?" he said, warily surveying the conventional patrons.

"Don't overanalyze."

"I need to at least commence analyzing before committing that crime."

"Don't bother."

John sighed. "So what is my purpose here in all this?"

"To witness the pureness of expression, the beauty of realizing…"

"In other words, to come to your aid if disaster strikes?"

Patrick was faintly amused.

"Perhaps Patrick, there are better places and times for this."

Vehemence instantly flooded Patrick's narrowed eyes. "Don't

lecture me about times or places," he said. He emptied his glass
and slammed it onto the table. "I was raised in a time and place
sealed from the slightest expression of any sort."

"My comment wasn't a lecture," John said. "Just some prudent advice."

Patrick seethed, his top lip trembling.

Most of the café was filled with couples, or small groups of
men and women. "So what exactly do you have planned here?"
John said.

"Rectitude."

John refilled his glass. "That's not overly specific."

"Have you bothered to ponder, for a moment, what it's like for
me?" Patrick said, his voice becoming shrill.

"I haven't spent inordinate amounts of time doing so, but yes,
I've considered your circumstances."

"Don't be sardonic," he said, dismissively waving his hand.

"That's not my intention, at least not my paramount one," John
said. "Have you been in contact with home?"

"To what end?" Patrick said laughing. "Derision? What is
wrong with you?"

Both remained silent for a time as voices buzzed within the café.

"As you know, my beloved family in Bordeaux isn't lacking
capital or property, just the flexibility requisite for humane, truth-
ful living."

"And this is where you chose to move for modern, liberal
thinking?"

"They don't ask certain questions here," Patrick said. "And
their identity is still forming, just like ours." He lifted his glass
for a toast and John acquiesced. Their glasses clinked delicately,
despite Patrick's condition.

"And now," Patrick said, standing, "to profess: to profess my
feelings."

John held his arm, but Patrick shirked himself away; he was fastened to his course. Patrick needed this moment, whatever the repercussions. "Best of luck with your professions," John said, bracing for the squall.

Patrick teetered across the room, struggling to balance past the other tables. He circled the far table, and placed a hand onto the tall man's shoulder, who looked up, confused. Patrick spoke to him, but John couldn't hear anything said. The tall man and the two other seated men and the woman were clearly perplexed, as they alternated between conferring and looking back at Patrick, who hadn't ceased speaking.

Patrick uttered something that he must have known would be flammable, for he retreated just before the tall man leapt up and grabbed him by the lapels of his blazer, ramming him against the glass-covered photos on the wall. The piercing sound of shattering glass momentarily froze the café.

John dashed across the room and hurled the man sideways off of Patrick. Patrick immediately flopped onto the floor. Someone restrained John's arms from behind and a sound blow landed on his cheek. He escaped the clutch and doled out punches of his own, a fair percentage converging with their intended destinations: the craniums of the nearby men. Chairs fell, screams, and Patrick remained on the floor alertly watching the activity. The clash recruited more participants who, albeit entirely unaware of the conflict's origin, were not loath to partaking in the melee.

After receiving and throwing more blows, John raised Patrick's limp body from the ground and dragged him outside, leaving behind a thriving tumult. They reached a cobblestone street beyond the café's view. The stones were sleek from a brief rain. John touched the tender side of his face where a heavy punch had landed. Patrick stood several feet away, propped against a wall and warily watching him. They remained silent for several moments.

"So these professions of yours, were they fruitful?" John asked.

Patrick gazed at his leather shoes, his head shaking side to side.

"For heaven's sake, are you happy with what you caused in there?" John demanded. "And might I also note what great help you were."

Patrick didn't respond. Scolding him was futile, so John exhaled and relaxed. "Do me one favor," John said, rubbing his face. "Please remind me not to answer your phone calls anymore."

"I'm sorry John," Patrick said through a meek smile. He was still leaning against the wall, his jacket moist and stained from the floor. He appeared smaller than usual.

"It's OK. Don't worry, it's fine," John said. "It was kind of fun. And I admire the way you immediately fell to the ground and just observed all the action, including me getting smacked, from that comfortable position." Patrick smiled, shaking his head. After patting him on his shoulder and placing him in a taxi, John said they would speak soon.

# Chapter 11

John lay on his hard bed. The rocklike mattress would dismay most, but he never noticed it. Faint sounds of scraping and dripping emerged from the rooms in his massive apartment, rooms he rarely bothered to enter.

The windows lacked curtains, but as he was on the topmost floor in the area he didn't mind. The ghastly moonlight allowed him to observe the deep lines on his palms. His fingertips stroked his swollen cheek but his mind was elsewhere.

"Alina is ridiculous," he thought.

She could be in a better situation. She should attain those promotions she spoke of. And her sitting alone at the opera was nonsense; she knew many people here, and, he felt it important to note, unlike him she was a reasonable person. She wasn't living his pathetic existence where he deserved his isolation. No need for her to be the same. Ridiculous.

Yet, he did need to consider her situation more carefully. For it might be true she met some resistance from those around her. Look at her darling grandmother. Alina lived what was, at least for here, an alternative model of living that did seem to extract the worst out of others.

Yes, it was true she didn't seem to receive the utmost encouragement from those around her. It was fair to say people weren't welcoming her with open arms. Cosmin spoke of her as if she were some sort of laboratory animal for study. Her talents and gifts were multifarious; people tend to both admire and to loathe this, the latter emotion often indefatigably concealed. And heaven forbid someone breaks the commonplace model, especially someone blessed like her; this inevitably leads to legions of threatened, defensive individuals. How dare you impugn their paradigm of living!

Times were arduous in this region. A country's escape from a festering regime does not lead to instantaneous revival, as is often comfortably believed by many cradling newspapers and reclining in armchairs in distant and better situations. Recovery is tortuous and burning, and has many agonizing setbacks. Many never make it through.

Yes, he needed to admit it was difficult for her.

But, at the same time, he sensed Alina could be more accommodating; she could alternate her dispositions. There were other viewpoints and strategies she could be implementing to improve her situation. He had seen many of those applied in the competitive working environments he had once been submerged in, and was acutely aware of them. He had a sense she was not. She struggled navigating through these times. Oh yes, there were many strategies she could employ, many things she could do. No need for her to have that kind of life.

His palm darkened as a cloud shrouded the moon. There was no need for her to have that kind of life.

Rumor was that the hotel opening party, situated in the lobby, would actually include quality drinks, not the conventional watered ale or bitter table wine. John's preparation, while limited, did encounter a few minor hurdles. He did polish his shoes, but not before first dashing out to purchase polish that he abruptly noticed he did not possess, for shining his shoes had not been the utmost priority in these last months. His fine evening blazer did take some time to locate, but upon discovering it he removed it from the plastic bag that entombed it.

The hotel was a few streets away on Strada Baba Novac. He had noted construction on the narrow building a few weeks previous, but hadn't realized it was completed. Alina's invitation to the party had surprised him, for their last interaction before her grandmother's building had hardly ended on what one would term a lofty note, but he accepted heartily and was eager to witness how she interacted with others and how they reacted to her. Much could be learned from this, as many of those attending would be her colleagues or others working in her field. The plan was to meet at the hotel at seven-thirty, and it was fifteen minutes past seven. After dunking his face into a sink brimming with frigid water he departed.

The chamber music, performed in the lobby's corner by a suited group of three with damp and neatly combed hair, reached into the street before the hotel. A fairly large and well-dressed crowd had already arrived. The bar was in the far corner, and tables of hors d'oeuvres near the entrance. Guests smiled and nodded at him as he passed. The aroma of the assorted perfumes morphed into one synthetic scent. Apparently this rather wealthy club accepted him, although he did not recognize anyone. Alina was still not in sight.

"So you are fashionably late?" Alina asked as he walked by. She stepped out from beside a window, where she had been standing alone. She cradled a flute of champagne with her slender fingers. As always, she was a remarkable sight.

"I will assume you watched me enter," John said.

"Of course."

"It's only one minute past seven-thirty," John said. "Perhaps one minute qualifies as late, but certainly not as fashionable."

She offered him a glass of champagne and mentioned the need to make an urgent work phone call. He would explore for a few minutes, as the party occupied several rooms. Alina exited the hotel while on the phone. He flowed through the crowd fairly comfortably as people actively engaged in conversation. A handsome man in his forties with a dark complexion and curly brown hair stepped forth from a group, and held out his hand before him. A cigarette balanced on his other hand.

"Andre," he said. "You are enjoying the affair?"

"Quite nice."

"I hope you like my hotel," he said, intensely gauging John's reaction.

The abrupt insertion of this substantial comment was intended to startle, as well as to induce praise. This Andre, proud of his work, enjoyed sampling the impact that his accomplishment had on others, and he watched John expectantly, his nascent smile craving to expand. It had little affect on John, but John saw no reason to resist the latter purpose. "Congratulations on your opening."

"And how do you like the place?"

"An excellent location."

"With a hotel, that is the essential."

"Absolutely."

"You are with an investment firm?" he asked.

A response dissuading further questions was needed. "I'm self-employed." Andre briskly nodded. In Eastern Europe, in the early nineties, when high levels of corruption still persisted, one didn't pursue information about the numerous cloaked careers of others. "I'd noticed your place a few weeks ago, but I didn't realize you were ready to open."

"But why?"

"The last time I passed the construction was incomplete."

"It is incomplete."

John hesitated. "But you are ready to open."

"No, we are not. At least these rooms appear finished."

John surveyed the attendees around him. "I see. But you have this opening party?"

Andre stepped towards John, exhaling a svelte strand of bluish smoke from the left corner of his mouth. "Everything for the party was already scheduled; invitations were sent out some time ago. We didn't want to cancel," he said. "It doesn't look good."

"Of course, I understand." John was sympathetic towards his situation, partially due to the fact that he candidly confessed to him, although John couldn't claim to be cognizant of why he did so. "So if not tomorrow, which day do you open?"

Andre sipped his drink. "Within a year, hopefully."

John successfully suppressed the impulse to spit up his champagne. Oddly though, Andre didn't seem to believe what he said was the least bit startling. He remained poised, his cigarette in his mouth.

"Well you do throw a fine party," John said, as two other men stepped in to speak with Andre and John walked away.

The relatively extensive scotch assortment at the bar was a surprise and a delight. He partook of a single malt variety possessing a robust, smoky flavor and aroma. Alina was still not in sight, but he assumed she had returned, and areas of the party were still uncharted.

The construction of the lobby appeared complete. The claret floor tiles gleamed, and the walls were freshly painted a pale green.

The reception desk, serving as the bar, was lined with a polished copper strip. Propped against this bar was a lumbering man coated by a tuxedo that appeared primed to burst. He pulled on a cigar while swirling his drink.

John recognized him from the Opera; he often prowled the entrance before shows.

"I've enjoyed La Boheme," John said.

The immense man looked at him, the tip of his cigar reddening.

"My most reliable customer," he said, patting John on the back. "We have never formally been introduced, although I feel I know you. Tibi," he said, shaking John's hand with his padded fingers.

John backed up slightly to evade the miasma of smoke. "I'll assume you are the manager of the theater?"

"You assume correctly." He eyed John's glass. "Excellent choice; it's nice to see a man with good taste. And I am also a fan of whiskeys. My collection comes from Scotland and Ireland, and I assure you, I visit them nightly." Tibi raised a plate burdened with a stack of salami and cheeses and vanquished the entire load within seconds. He absorbed the slices, abandoning the customary chewing and swallowing. The hairs on his auburn beard overhanging his mouth were yellowish, discolored from smoking.

So here was the man Lavinia had referred to backstage, the heartless "he" who was oppressing all those who worked at the theater. "How is business at the theater?" John asked.

He lowered the bare plate. "You should know."

"The audience is usually sparse."

"True," Tibi said lugubriously, staring into his russet drink. "Hopefully some interest in our endeavors will one day arise in this city. The people here, they have little excitement."

This sad facial expression, unduly embellished, must be a useful little tool of his. "As a general prescript," John said, "people have difficulty becoming excited about things they don't know exist."

"Oh?" Tibi said. The mournful display instantly terminated, replaced by a barely concealed vehemence.

John swirled his whiskey. He proceeded deliberately, allowing Tibi's vitriol to ferment to a higher proof. "Perhaps this is a radical idea, but maybe some advertisement, using all those city and federal subsidies you receive, would help a bit," John said. "Curiously, I've never seen one poster or any notification for any of the productions anywhere in this city."

Tibi's face reddened with his cigar. "We do what we can."

"I've had the pleasure of meeting some of the cast, and they mentioned times are very difficult for them," John said, scanning Tibi's pressed tuxedo. He prudently avoided names. "Quite a shame for them. But hopefully, as you said, more interest will arise." John extended his hand, and after observing it with repugnance, Tibi shook it brusquely.

Alina was seated on a leather chair at the far side of the adjoining room. Her sleek black dress extended to just above her knees. Her legs were crossed and she grasped a champagne flute with both hands.

"How nice to see you," she said to John.

"Why did you ask me to come here at seven-thirty?"

"What's wrong with seven-thirty?"

"With the numbers, nothing. With the time, I overheard things started at six."

Alina turned away. "No need to be prickly."

"I agree. I'm just curious why you asked me to arrive an hour and a half late?"

"I actually avoided the first ninety minutes as well, although I admit I would have liked to avoid this entirely. Now I'm just getting in a little socializing."

John surveyed the emptiness in her immediate vicinity. "You're performing superbly."

Alina turned back to John, the corner of her mouth upturned. "And you?"

"I had the pleasure of meeting the loveable Mr. Tibi, who's the manager of the theater."

"I've unfortunately seen him."

"I believe I know where the money supposedly going to the theater is vanishing to. Ticket sales are few, but the city and state give the theater a stipend, and I don't believe our dear Mr. Tibi is investing it there."

"That's not a surprise," Alina said.

"It's not, but it would make quite a difference if it were used for its original intention." John said. "I'm sure the cast and orchestra would concur."

The crowd milled before them. "Who invited you to this party?"

"I know a good share of people here."

"Excellent. So why don't we consort a bit with your good share?" he said, motioning to the crowd.

"Why bother? We can chat right here."

"There is no statute preventing us from communicating while talking with others," John said, his arm extended towards the people. He was intent upon watching Alina interact.

As they walked through the crowd, the influence of the champagne and drinks was apparent. Hands reclined on shoulders belonging to people normally abhorred, and laughter rolled out a bit more boisterously than the anecdotes warranted. As John followed slightly behind, Alina curtly acknowledged several men who said hello with expectant faces, and she continued steadily forward, leaving them frozen in her wake. A balding man, who likely wasn't as old as his retreating hairline suggested, seized her arm.

"Long time," he said.

She, with a snapping flex, liberated her arm from his grip and looked at John. "This is my friend John. From New York."

The man, Sergiu, observed John from shoes to hair. "Well, well, well."

John, amused, was not sure exactly how Sergiu expected him to respond to his absurd utterance.

"So John, what brings you to this part of the world?" he asked.

"I heard about this lovely party."

Sergiu was astonished, his mouth an oval, and then he snapped into laughter, stamping once and raising his glass. "I own a real estate office on Avram Iancu."

His mentioning of his office was entirely unprompted and ludicrously out of context. But he was exorbitantly proud and his chest puffed. Apparently he would have mentioned it regardless of the direction of the conversation. "Excellent," John said.

"You are involved with real estate?" he asked John.

"No."

After a few moments of silence, Sergiu realized no more information was forthcoming, and he saluted. He now exhibited a penchant for John, sliding alongside him and facing Alina. "I wish you and your investment company wouldn't be so terrified of bringing us some business," Sergiu said to her, playfully winking at John. "A little courage in life helps." He winked again and elbowed John during the ensuing silence. John looked down at his champagne flute.

"Unfortunately I have an outlandish tendency when advising my company," Alina said. "I suggest investing in well-run and profitable ventures."

Sergiu didn't orally respond, but his neck veins emerged and all winking ceased. His hairline seemed to ebb even farther back. Attempting to diminish the unpleasantness, John suggested a visit to the well-stocked bar, but it wasn't to be that easy. Sergiu's brittle ego had been defiled and a man that fragile always needs immediate retribution.

"Forgive me if I put any pressure on you," Sergiu said to Alina. "But of course you're only an assistant manager." He turned to John. "You see, in fairness to Alina, I should be discussing this with someone in a position of consequence, and not wasting my time."

The response would be interesting.

"Considering the condition of your business, you would be wasting your time discussing it with anyone," Alina said. "That is, of course, unless your purpose is to be humiliated."

She walked away, smiling, and John said farewell to the effigy of Sergiu. They met at the bar. So her people skills might not be her paramount talent.

"What was that?" John asked.

Alina laughed. "He deserved it."

"Oh he absolutely did. And you undoubtedly gave it to him. But that's how you promote your reputation?"

"I'm not running for mayor."

"Thank God," John said, "or the City Hall would have mass suicides."

Alina laughed, holding John's hand. "Don't be so uptight. I'm accustomed to making sure these people get what they deserve. They deserve it. And from what you mentioned earlier, I don't think you exactly charmed Tibi."

"You're certainly right there. But I'm not the one desperate for a promotion in this town."

"Desperate?" Alina asked, whisking her hand away. "And how do you arrive at *desperate*? Is there anything wrong with getting what I earned?"

"Not that I'm aware of."

Alina stepped closer to John. "Look, those I work with know what I can do. And my reputation hasn't escaped others. But I remain an assistant, with others taking credit and getting promoted for what I kill myself for." Alina's jaw muscles pulsed. "And then I get these attitudes."

"So why would you believe others, outside your company, are aware of what you can do?"

"People talk," Alina said. "Why do you think Sergiu was asking for my help? He did so in a degrading manner, because he's a spineless imp who's too proud to directly ask. But he was begging for my help, believe me."

She was right. "Of course society is threatened by you," John said. "But let's be honest: at this point you must just accept that and proceed from there. And if your goal is rising in the business, you are not employing the wisest tactics to attain that goal."

"And you know all about this?"

"One thing I can say I have seen, and seen plenty of all my life, is people ascending the hierarchy. The successful ones, when dealing with the people in their workplace and field, always employ a balance of aggressiveness and prudence. It's no easy task."

Alina rested her hand against her hip, and her hand was clenched. "So what is it you think I'm doing?"

John monitored the hand. "Venting your justifiable frustration. Either ignoring these people or soundly thrashing them. And I must confess it's an absolute pleasure to watch you in action due to your talent, and because they undoubtedly deserve it, as you say. But engaging in these petty battles will only hinder your path."

"Can you blame me?"

"No," John said, "I actually can't. Nonetheless, it will only harm your chances. Now obviously with your delightful grandmother, and I'm sure with your friends, you know how to restrain yourself." John looked around them. "But they're not the ones affecting your career. Please heed this: amassing a trail of humiliated colleagues who are unaccustomed to being insulted, especially by a woman who knows far more than they, won't leave you with a fan base eager to propel you forward."

Alina's eyes were glassy as she stared at the crowd. Her hands hung limply at her sides. John knew nothing more could be accomplished now, and it was time to move on.

"But this is a party. Let us make some use of that fact," he said, reaching over the bar and grabbing an unopened champagne bottle from a bucket of ice.

# Chapter 12

The snowy landscape was pristine. The flakes, intricate and soft, had ceased falling an hour ago. The sun had just risen but the area was still silent. Lofty rows of wild chestnut trees fortified both sides of the wide path that ran through the middle of Parcul Central. With no one present, and with the early rays of the sun gleaming off the unblemished whiteness, the path seemed an ethereal link to beyond. John focused on this brightness and was drawn towards it. He rued the footprints he left for he didn't want to alter this image in any fashion.

John's breath was cotton in the biting air. Wearing a dark woolen coat and scarf, and rubbing his gloved hands together, he stepped softly in the light snow. The bark of a nearby tree was coated with pale powder, and the slender ends of the branches, devoid of leaves, were encapsulated in ice. He removed his glove, licked his fingertip, and slid it along the smooth, clear coating; it glided effortlessly.

A fluttering of wings erupted overhead, and three robins circled the tree. After they perched, John gently stepped back from the trunk to observe, but was dismayed as they launched in response to his minor movement. He remained motionless, his breath freezing in clouds before him, wishing for their return. Eventually two robins landed on branches a few feet above, and their red coats contrasted sharply with the pallid bark and the ivory sky. He didn't breathe. After darting their heads about canvassing the surroundings, the robins floated down the path and vanished into the light.

John moved towards the Somes River. He had not visited it in weeks, and he was curious if any of these steady Romanian fishermen practiced their art in this weather. Every time he had been to the river they had been present, and their reliability was reassuring. The river's edges were now frozen. Both sides were snow-covered ice, with water winding through the narrowed center. No fishermen stood along the immediate banks, but bare elm trees slept along the inclines.

John's phone was turned off. He didn't want to consciously ignore calls, to have to consider each person each time he disregarded them, so he had closed his phone three days ago. It was the easier way, to just seal off contact. It was also the cowardly way. And he had ignored the knocks on his door.

This behavior differed from his recent course. In the last weeks he had made efforts to visit places and interact with others. It had not been easy or wholly pleasant, but he resisted his instincts and had made the effort. He had attended the hotel party a week ago, and spoke with Alina on the phone for two evenings afterwards. But the compulsion to retreat into the silence and isolation he was accustomed to had assaulted him ruthlessly and without any specific prompting, and he capitulated to these temptations.

His interactions with others, albeit a bit trying, had been generally positive, and speaking with Alina was engrossing, but he needed some time to revert back to being by himself. He sought to shatter this need, but his current isolation was necessary. Reading his books and staring out his windows lost in inebriated thought were the primary activities of the last days.

No fishermen were to be seen as he walked along the river, and he was disheartened. Cluj was awakening: cars, their cylinders starving for fuel in the cold, struggled to start, and pedestrians scuttled along, heads down to keep warm. After half a mile, in a hushed area, the river angled and widened. Across the banks, where the frosted rocks reached out farthest into the ice, two elderly fishermen in dark coats and high rubber boots had strung their fishing lines beyond the ice, and moved their poles gradually from side to side. So the weather did not stop them. How commendable. The fishermen didn't speak to each other, but moved simultaneously. John waited for a time to see if a fish was pulled from the icy water, but of course not one emerged.

After passing an empty sport park filled with tall, snowy pines, and moving past several desolate river banks, John was relieved to happen upon another fisherman standing along the ice. His pole lay in the snow and he stared at the river before him. John believed he recognized him, but only proximity could verify this suspicion.

The man didn't turn as John approached. Either he had been undetected, or his approach didn't arouse interest. At several feet away, John was sure he knew him; they had shared sunflower seeds by the river months ago. He was pleased to find him again. John debated what to say, but decided a concise "hello" would suffice. During his prior encounter he recalled that the fisherman could not be branded as loquacious. John shifted in the snow, and the fisherman gradually turned. He appeared confused, looking from John to the water. This confusion was contagious, as John forgot to utter the planned hello, instead studying the man's crimson-veined eyes in silence. Eventually, the fisherman's countenance crinkled into a splendid smile of recognition, prompting John's wayward "hello".

The fisherman didn't delay in celebrating their reunion. He removed, from his coat, a label-free glass bottle filled with transparent liquid. After glancing at John, he raised it a foot above his face and poured a tight stream directly into his mouth, snapping the bottle back to a vertical position, not a drop misemployed. He handed John the bottle, and nodded in encouragement. The liquid's sour odor penetrated; it was the local palinca. This formidable alcohol was fermented from plums harvested in countryside orchards and was far more potent than any of the many hard alcohols John had encountered in his past, and let it be said there had been no shortage of samplings through the years. If John was to attempt this feat, and he certainly had his misgivings, he wanted to perform properly. He raised the bottle, lined up the tip with his mouth, inhaled, and poured. The stream met its destination, and he momentarily rejoiced, but as he raised the bottle to halt the flow, some splashed across his nose and forehead. The fisherman gently laughed. John endeavored to ignore the burn of the palinca in his mouth and throat, and he struggled to refrain from coughing the alcohol onto the snow. He was at least successful in the latter endeavor, although his alimentary canal was afire. After wiping his eyes with the back of his glove, he returned the bottle, and was rewarded by a bag of sunflower seeds from the admiring fisherman.

When the fisherman returned his attention to the river, John followed his gaze. The ice extended farther out in this section, the water flowing through the center a narrow brook.

John's thoughts, as he watched the water, meandered back to New York. He hadn't contacted anyone there for months. He rarely considered his former life anymore; if any thought did escape, he immediately extinguished it.

"I actually met people over the last several weeks; I started conversing with people again," John said.

The fisherman nodded. He would listen no matter what John

said, yet John had the decency to attempt to keep it coherent, or at least terse. He stopped, and pressed his foot deeper into the snow. "But of course I'm back to seclusion again." A cracking sound resonated from the river's center, as an ice block freed itself and washed downstream. "At least I'm out here today."

They watched the ice float away.

"Shall we," John said, pointing to the fishing pole.

The fisherman looked towards his fishing pole lying in the snow. He lifted it, dusting it off meticulously and deftly adjusting the reel. He stepped forward and cast the hook and line across the ice. It plunked emphatically into the frigid water.

John had some misgivings about his question, but he could not resist inquiring about what he had been wondering: "Are you expecting to catch anything?"

The fisherman's face crinkled again in a smile. That was his answer. John was contented to stay with him, and when he offered John an opportunity to fish, John hesitated, but upon the fisherman's insistence he accepted. It was not an overly complicated endeavor, which is why he was amused that he felt nervous about undertaking the task. The fisherman was satisfied, for he looked away from John and back to the river.

When the sun reached its apex, John thanked the fisherman for his company and headed home. And he was certain to turn on his phone while walking back.

"So you're answering now?" Alina demanded.

"Answering?" John said, as he distanced the phone from his ear to preserve his hearing.

"Your phone. You've finally decided to answer?"

"I believe our present conversation is evidence of that."

After weathering a few caustic comments, he agreed to meet Alina for lunch at a new sandwich shop near her office. He arrived at one o'clock, their designated time. It was on the narrow and desolate Strada Virgil Fulicea, on which was located only one other store, a tiny shop dedicated solely to the repair of dolls. John read the hanging wooden sign several times to be sure this place actually existed. He was fascinated and wondered how they functioned. It was then he noticed the door was shut, and the quaint wooden windows were dusty and curtained. Perhaps they had not survived.

He found the sandwich shop and noted through the glass door that it was empty. It had opened a week ago, and the middle-aged couple behind the counter, wearing starched aprons and looking anxiously about, were assuredly the owners. They were possessed by the edginess difficult to exorcise after a business opening, and their feverish condition would remain for another few weeks. Then they would begin to dart around less, realizing that nothing was gained by incessant movement.

Sandwiches were ordered at the clean white counter, which were then served at the few round tables. These tables were freshly wiped and adorned with cylindrical oil and vinegar containers filled to their brims. The floor was damp from mopping. John sat and waited for Alina. The owner materialized, his bald head as polished as the tables, and through a smile stretched to daunting proportions, he asked John what he would like to order. John informed him he was waiting for someone, and the man's face contorted as he struggled for words, until he finally said it was absolutely fine for him to wait, that it was absolutely no problem in any way, he could wait as long as he wished. He then attempted to appear busy by vigorously wiping the spotless counter.

Alina entered, wearing a sand-colored business suit and carrying a valise over her shoulder. She sat beside John.

"We should order at the counter," John said.

The menu, far from extensive, included six sandwich variations inscribed on a white board hanging above the counter. As they discussed it, the owner's fidgeting escalated with the passing seconds. His wife, a stocky woman perhaps half his height and double his weight, glared at him from the side. By any standards, she was a harrowing sight. After glancing at her, her husband exclaimed in an exasperated voice that if they didn't find something to their liking, he could prepare any combination that pleased them. John mollified him by immediately ordering.

"Do you think they'll survive?" Alina asked, looking around the room from their table.

"I'm afraid they won't. Not only is this location fairly well hidden, but this is something new in Cluj, similar to a western fast food place. It takes time to get used to this concept."

Plates clanked, utensils dropped, and the man pleaded a few times from the back as the sandwiches were prepared.

"They are also lacking some key qualities of a fast food place," John said.

"Such as?"

"The 'fast'."

"Let us also not forget that people around here are accustomed to purchasing their own bread and fillings, and making sandwiches themselves," Alina said.

"You should give everyone some advice."

"And say what — Ladies and Gentlemen, from this point onward flexibility in life is permitted, and making your own lunches is no longer requisite — I wish it were that simple."

Ten minutes later, both owners, still behind the counter, placed the sandwiches on a tray and scrutinized them. The woman barked at her husband, propelling him towards the table with the offerings. After their deliverance, he stepped back to admire his work.

John did not look, but surmised from the abrupt end to the

turmoil behind the counter that the owners were studying them, attempting to glean information.

"You still haven't explained to me why you didn't answer your phone for days," Alina said. "I haven't forgotten to ask you."

"Apparently not," John said, continuing to eat. "I couldn't answer it."

"What happened?" She appeared concerned, and had yet to sample her food.

"It was turned off."

Alina was not amused, and emphatically bit into her fastidiously assembled lunch. An explanation was imperative. "I'm not sure why I turned everything off."

"So something was wrong?"

"Oh, absolutely."

"What?"

"Well," John said, "I don't fully know the answer to that. Rancid memories, a rotten existence. I'm not sure. But as you see, for better or worse, I have returned to this planet."

The owner was beside the table, his arms painted to his sides, and he inquired about the food. Alina satisfied his hunger for endorsement by offering words of praise. He nodded and thanked them twice before being subjected to a series of questions in the back room.

A short man with a puffy dark jacket entered the restaurant but halted beside the door when spotting Alina. Alina didn't notice. He looked back and forth from Alina to John with sharp twists of his neck, then shuffled to the counter with his meagre legs. Alina watched him pass.

"That's Voicu," she said. "He works as a sort of administrator at the company; fairly low level. He's originally from a small mountain village in the Maramures region. But he's in full charge of all gossip."

Voicu stood with his side to the counter, enabling himself to watch Alina and John while maintaining what he erringly believed to be a casual posture.

"Observe," Alina said. "Voicu!"

Voicu turned to her with a distorted look of surprise that would be considered exorbitant in a daytime television drama.

"I hadn't noticed you," Voicu said.

"That's understandable considering the immensity of the place."

Voicu blushed. Although rigorously studying John before, undoubtedly harvesting for his impending office gossip installment, he couldn't even glance at him now that he had been announced and John directly faced him.

"Voicu, it's nice to meet you," John said.

Voicu turned with affected surprise. He wore an even more embellished expression than his first, although this had previously seemed unachievable. A timid hello emerged from his barely open mouth.

When he left, Alina shook her head. "He'll be reporting this at the office within minutes."

"What is there to report?"

"Oh, he'll contrive plenty. Have faith. They're ravenous for any gossip about me, and he's afraid to disappoint."

John finished his sandwich. It was time to ask about her work, about how things were progressing, but a precarious topic it was. He exhaled. "So what is happening with the job?"

"Meaning what?" Alina crisply replied, placing both hands onto the table, her thumbs encircling one another.

John warily considered whether the displayed hands, more proximate to him now, were placed there in order to reduce the journey to the side of his face. "You had mentioned possible promotions. The Vice President resigning."

Alina looked at the leftovers on her plate. "Forget about all that."

"How can I forget about what I don't know?"

"Just switch subjects."

"I'm curious about what is happening."

Alina's hands squeezed together. "What is wrong with you?"

John glanced at the ceiling and back at Alina. "Marvelous question. Marvelous. But I don't want to take too much of your time."

"Why are you intent on pursuing this?" Alina said. The crinkling alongside her eyes revealed her anguish.

He had been eager to hear more about her work situation and offer possible strategies. Just moments ago, he had relinquished some of his resistance and attempted to answer her personal questions, but she was reluctant to do the same. Although frustrated, he didn't want to induce further distress. "Yes, forget that," he said. "Let me go pay."

At the counter, the sturdy woman received the money, but looked up at John with horror upon realizing they didn't possess proper change for the bill. She shrieked, and her husband exploded out from the back door and ran in circles with a frenetic pace that would shame a headless chicken, and then told John he would sprint down the street and find change. John assured him that that would be unnecessary, for he would return tomorrow for the change and to order again.

Several days later, John and Alina strolled through a chilly afternoon. Although the day was bright with an unobstructed blue sky, sharp cold predominated. Some of the side streets, hidden amidst quiet portions of the city center, were narrow enough that John mused certain vehicles could not squeeze through. Many magnificent buildings on these lanes, moss and lichen covered, were several hundred years old and crumbling and calling for repair. How startling the city would be with a renovation of its architecture.

Alina remained silent as they walked side by side. She appeared to be measuring her thoughts, weighing whether raising them would be advisable. John buttressed himself for what lie ahead.

"You work hard at discussing me with me," Alina said.

It was an inauspicious beginning. "Quite ineffective labor."

"We shouldn't ignore talking about you."

"I can't accuse you of doing that."

The streets were dense with the afternoon crowd. Two blocks away was the Piata Mihai Viteazul, where a vast fruit and vegetable market thrived during the lunch hour, and many passing by contentedly toted heavy bags and cradled batches of white carrots or bundles of fresh spinach.

"You don't work anymore," Alina said.

He instantly considered derailing the conversation, due not only to his aversion to discussing himself, but to Alina's resistance lately to talking about her work. Yet he chose to counteract his initial instinct, and to give a little. Someone needed to.

"Really?"

"But you don't."

"I don't work at my prior career anymore," John said.

"So you are working?"

Three gypsy children crowded near an elderly woman who sat on a bench, her cloth grocery sack beside her. "I'm working to learn," John said.

Alina appeared a trifle confused. "What?"

"I read and research topics I never studied before, works and subjects I have always ignored. That's my work at present."

Alina considered this. "And money?"

"Money I did well with before," John said. "It was the only thing I was successful at. And I barely spend anything. You see, the wine is not that expensive."

Alina halted before a brittle, three-story apartment building. The ashen plaster façade was cracking from time and the elements. John scanned the building, tracing a fissure upwards. "My questions trouble you?" Alina said.

"I don't believe my answer will deter you either way."

The three gypsy children were now beside the woman's grocery sack, but she didn't notice. The shortest of them eased nearer. He casually reached towards it. John was unsure whether to intercede, for a skirmish could result and the children might then choose to plague him. As the child looked away from the bag, his hand vanished inside it. John shouted. All three instinctively leapt and fled. They were efficient: there was no reason to persist, for they would easily find targets without hassle elsewhere. The woman never noticed a thing. She remained sitting with an impassive expression, her hands folded on her lap.

"I'm impressed," Alina said. "So how did you spot that?"

"Unfortunately for me, I tend to notice a lot."

As they continued to walk, Alina rubbed her hands together while blowing into them. They paused beside a store entirely dedicated to honey and honey products. Dozens of glass jars were carefully stacked in spires by the window, and the colors of their contents ranged from white to amber, each jar seeking attention.

"So what made you leave work?"

"I told you, I am working."

"Your career. What made you leave your career?"

One jar atop a stack was filled with an incandescent honey that appeared particularly appetizing. Alina awaited her answer. Her tone was determined as she had planned this questioning for days. What greatly intrigued him was that he discovered he didn't mind answering questions as much when Alina was the inquirer. "First of all, your question assumes that leaving my career was entirely my choice," John said.

"Meaning what?"

John took a last look at the honey. "Meaning I was arrested for illegal trading practices."

Alina stared, waiting. The sole of her shoe scraped the pavement. What to say and how to say it were nebulous. The stillness grew uncomfortable, and she pressed forth: "What happened?"

"That's what happened. That was it," John said. "I got off with sanctions and no jail. And the truth be told, I could have gone back to work after waiting for a while. Almost all of my rampant success was before I became involved with those activities towards the end. The opportunity was there for me to return to the industry, but I did not want to return."

"How do you explain that?"

"I normally don't."

A stout young man with a reddened face and an ill-fitting suit hustled down the street, panting. His gray pants were worn at the knees, and excessive space lingered between his jacket and chest. He likely had borrowed the suit from an extremely portly relative for a new job. He attempted to consume a sandwich while moving, and half a sausage dropped onto the sidewalk. The man looked upwards and implored the heavens, a reaction seemingly disproportionate to the loss, and continued on his way, a deeper shade of red.

"Aren't people supposed to have our type of discussion in a tranquil locale, perhaps by a lake?" John asked. "Maybe swans?"

Alina was faintly amused.

"You must understand, I was a product of a streamlined system," John said. "Business and finance is all I ever did, from the start."

"That doesn't seem so horrible."

"You're right, it doesn't seem so," John said. "But it was."

Alina looked at him with curiosity. "Shouldn't you be returning to work now?" he said.

"No."

John laughed. "Perhaps a clearer answer?"

"I just don't see what was so horrible."

They passed an elderly man grasping a bottle partially covered by a stained paper bag that assuredly was not employed to conceal a soda. "Have I mentioned I have partaken of the local palinca? One must be braced for its bite," John said.

Alina didn't want the conversation to veer off track. She anticipated receiving a certain amount of information, and failing to do so this time would be unacceptable. They walked in the direction of her office. The sun's rays heated John's skin.

"What you were doing seems perfectly understandable," Alina said.

"Perhaps, but it becomes a problem when you ignore everything else and care for nothing else. Forget about evolving," John said, "as a putrefying devolution actually occurs."

They walked in silence. Alina took her time to absorb and analyze this. "So I must ask why then do you encourage my success in this business world if you are so against it?"

"I'm not. I'm opposed to any world or career or lifestyle where one loses sight of everything and becomes a selfish and destructive bastard. One doesn't notice it happening until it's too late. It's very easy to do, please trust me, a veritable expert at it."

John checked the time. He reminded Alina that she had to leave, although she yearned to remain. For the first time, as she stared at him and mulled over what he had said, she appeared vulnerable, and John was moved by this susceptibility.

"Let's talk later," she said.

"Of course."

"With you that's not a guarantee."

"The 'of course' is guaranteed," John said. "But how far the definition of 'later' can be stretched is often the portion ripe for debate."

She kissed his cheek, her hair brushing against his eyes, and walked away. He dabbed the thin layer of dampness on his forehead and steadied his breathing. Alina approached her workplace entrance with long, firm steps. Her dark hair contrasted against her jacket. Another group, perhaps employees of her company, arrived at the same time. They clogged the doorway. Alina was taller than most of them, and she glided through to the doors. She didn't seem to notice them, although several of them looked up at her as she passed.

# Chapter 13

John walked down Strada Clinicilor towards Babes University. He brushed against the buildings to avoid the rickety Dacia automobiles that roared through the tight one-way road. The cars were still too close for comfort, particularly since some drivers were more fixated on the chunks of fresh bread they masticated than on the narrow street before them.

Cosmin had requested, multiple times, for John to attend one of his lectures, and John replied that it would be a redundant undertaking since he weathered these orations each time they met. This snub, of course, didn't dissuade Cosmin, for after the minor delay of narrowing his eyes and smirking, he plunged back into imploring John to visit the class he taught biweekly. After taking several years off, he was now working on his doctorate degree, and lecturing undergraduates in beginning courses was a step in the process.

John's scarf was bundled around his neck and he lowered his chin into its warmth as he ascended a hill on the main campus. The paved paths were lined with bare elm trees, and browned lawns separated the old university buildings. Students spiritedly

117

rustled about in small groups, holding sacks and piles of books. No matter what he would endure in Cosmin's class, the journey through campus was at least pleasurable. Cosmin had insisted he would enjoy the subject matter, and John concurred that he most certainly would, it was its delivery that prompted his trepidation. Today's lecture was from two o'clock to three-twenty, and it was now ten minutes to three.

John located the history faculty, passing through its stone facade and climbing the worn stairs to the second floor. Loosening his scarf would be unnecessary as it was only slightly warmer inside. Would the students be partaking in a group slumber during the lecture? That was a distinct possibility. Cosmin was in an amphitheater style classroom with one hundred iron and wooden folding seats that had been installed seventy years ago. The room was three-quarters full, and Cosmin had a sprawling chalkboard at his disposal that he was not hesitant to use.

Fortunately the entrance was at the top; only a few heads turned to see John enter, but one could not misinterpret the jubilance on Cosmin's face. He strove to avoid looking at John and continue his lecture unimpeded, but his eyes darted over several times. Cosmin's elocution, already animated, became more enlivened, and he paced the floor with a spring to each step. John sat near the doorway and watched with curiosity. Cosmin spoke about the effects of communism in the rural workplace in Eastern Europe, and although he continued to strive not to do so, he gauged John's reaction every few moments. John could not suppress a smile provoked by the level of satisfaction Cosmin experienced due to his presence.

It should be noted that the students were actually attentive. They reacted with glee at Cosmin's humorous anecdotes, and appeared perturbed when he spoke of disturbing events. In truth he lectured effectively, and it was a notable display. It dawned on John that he should not be surprised, since Cosmin was well-read and zealous. And he certainly practiced enough during his free time. Also a fresh element existed to the lecture that John needed time to determine: Cosmin spoke, and John listened, without the influence of red wine. Truly this was an exceptional occasion.

When the class emptied, John descended to the front row and sat, stretching his legs. Cosmin remained on the lecture floor, his hands on his hips, mouth slightly open, eagerly awaiting a reaction. He could not wait long.

"So?"

"Do you write their exams?" John asked.

Cosmin's arms relaxed. "Oh yes, I certainly do. Sadly for them."

John surveyed the high ivory-colored ceiling above and Cosmin began erasing the massive accumulation of chalk. "I was surprised to see you here," he said, over his shoulder.

"I was also." John was glad he visited, for as is typically the case, when one finally comes around and undertakes what has been repeatedly neglected, a rewarding experience follows. He had even detected the warmth of pride for Cosmin while observing him performing in his classroom. The smooth sound of the eraser gliding down the board had a tranquilizing effect, but the crack of a shutting door broke this peace. One of the students, with lengthy brown hair and violet eye shadow, marched down into the classroom.

"Can I help you, Ms. Hasek?" Cosmin asked, ceasing his activity.

Reaching the bottom of the room, she flashed a smile at John. Cosmin glanced at him. She said she didn't need any help and had simply left her pen in the classroom. She searched the chairs beside John. He had noticed her staring at him when he'd first entered. Cosmin watched uncomfortably, and recommenced erasing.

"You misplaced your pen?" John asked.

Her eye shadow fluttered. "Yes," she said. "Is it beside you?"

Cosmin's stiff figure cleared the board. "Considering that during class I sat near the highest row, and you sat near me, I doubt the pen cascaded all the way down to here, the bottom of the classroom," John said. "No disrespect to gravity intended."

Her face colored at John's comment.

"If I locate this essential pen, I'll be sure to save it for you," Cosmin said, looking at John as she marched out of the classroom.

"Tough," Cosmin said, laughing, "considering she came back to see you."

"Your class obviously enjoyed your lecture," John said. "As did I."

Cosmin's face brightened magnificently. "I'm happy to hear that John." He spoke in an earnest tone John was unaccustomed to hearing from him. "Very happy." He stepped forward. "We should celebrate tonight."

"Exactly what are we celebrating now?" John asked, fully aware that a consequential reason, or any reason, was not compulsory for Cosmin to declare a celebration.

"Wine. I just received a batch from my uncle's village in the Banat region near the Bihor Mountains in the south. It's not bad at all. I'll bring some tonight?"

Stark treetops were sharply visible through the elongated wooden framed windows.

"Sure."

John peered out into the sleek darkness. Cosmin would arrive soon. His thoughts drifted back to Alina, something that was transpiring with rising frequency.

She was desperate to change her present situation, but didn't want to discuss her potential promotions. She ached for them, but absolutely no discussion permitted. Yet who could blame her? It was agonizing to talk about. All her attributes, which others would rejoice possessing even a minute percentage of, led her to nowhere. She was imprisoned in positions just high enough that her talents could be exploited, yet not elevated enough to allow her to receive recognition or benefits.

Of course she didn't want to talk about it. Why bring up a ceaseless tribulation?

One reason would be to find solutions. He believed these solutions existed, but to help, he would need to examine this with her, and her resistance was frustrating.

Alina had accused him of avoiding discussing himself. She had been the only one with the mettle to say this directly to him. But lately he had begun to open up to her.

Yes, he thought about Alina with increasing frequency, and he wanted to know more about her, details about her. Did she add milk to her tea? What sort of films did she enjoy, and what was she paging through in bed at night? It had been some time since he thought of someone for longer than the duration he spent with her. In fact, it had been a long time since he thought of someone while he was with her.

He would telephone her now. He desired to hear her voice. She would inevitably ask questions about him, and push for answers. Oddly, he didn't dread these questions as much anymore. When they spoke he would discuss a variety of things, even himself. Maybe he would invite her out for lunch tomorrow, perchance even for dinner. This scenario suddenly engulfed him in an undulating apprehension. His phone rang.

"Doing anything productive?" Alina asked.

The call was unanticipated. "Yes, as a matter of fact. Testing the comfort level of my apartment chairs."

She laughed.

"Have you returned from work?" John said.

"I'm home now, but I still have plenty to do."

John recalled his old schedules in New York. Work was all there was time for. Perhaps occasional sleep. He wanted to ask her to join him for dinner tomorrow, but an alien emotion saturated him. After analysis, he identified it: shyness. But why this sudden shyness? He had spent time with her before. What in heavens was happening to him?

What he now contemplated was asking her on what society generally classifies as "a date". His shyness might be a propitious sign. Anything different about him must be a positive sign, he considered, laughing dryly.

"What are you doing after work tomorrow?" John said, his voice slightly askew.

"Leaving the office."

She could not be accused of making this easier. "And after you have completed your exit of the premises," John said, "why don't we meet?"

"Because we haven't made plans."

No, it wasn't easy. "Well let me remedy that. We can meet at Casa Alba for dinner."

Someone was knocking at John's door; Cosmin must have arrived. But why was Alina still silent? He had been foolish, irrational. She still did not speak. He should have waited until another time to ask her. He should have waited. The knocking persisted. That damned knocking.

"I'll see you there tomorrow night," Alina said.

When John opened the door, Cosmin was greeted with an ebullient shoulder pat. He hesitated, bemused, for he was unaccustomed to any form of greeting from John, and certainly not an amiable one. He toted several two liter plastic bottles filled with deep magenta fluid.

"May I introduce you to the product of my uncle's village," Cosmin said, placing the bottles on the living room table. "They make these yearly at the festival from locally grown grapes. And now we are the fortunate recipients of them."

John brought in wine glasses from the pantry. The living room was haunted by pointed shadows ascending the high walls; two tiny lamps on low tables lit the capacious space.

"Let us indulge in the vintage of their labor," Cosmin said.

The wine, of low alcohol content, smelled like sweet grape juice and tasted the same. One would not deem it a complex wine, but it was effortless to imbibe and anything would taste lovely at the moment.

"What do you think?" Cosmin said, holding up the glass.

"Wonderful Cosmin, just wonderful."

Cosmin looked at him with curiosity. "Well you certainly seem in high spirits."

Tomorrow evening at dinner John would ask Alina about these countryside wines.

Cosmin emptied his glass in a single pour. "I'm glad you enjoyed my lecture today," he said, falling into an expectant silence, his eyebrows subtly raised.

"I did, and your students undoubtedly did."

"Yes, and they are in the process of reforming."

John squinted.

"They are less corrupt," Cosmin explained.

John placed his glass onto the oaken table.

"Perhaps this may surprise you, but many professors and students have been corrupt for years," Cosmin said. He had detected John's interest, and accordingly spoke with enhanced deliberation. "Students often cheat on exams. But beyond that, they pay professors to raise their grades. This is common."

"Common?"

"Extremely. It was not even frowned on by anyone for a long time."

"Really."

"Oh yes," Cosmin continued, pleased with John's attention. "Professors calculated their income based on the bribes students gave them. These bribes weren't even much, but numerous. Parents often provided their children with the bribe money."

John refilled his glass with the alcohol-laced grape juice.

"You are enjoying my uncle's wine?"

"You said students are 'reforming'?"

Cosmin laughed, looking at John affectionately. "I always appreciate that you are concerned," he said, "as much as it might appear otherwise."

"I simply asked what you meant."

"The previous two years are the first where I've seen a decline in these practices. The younger, newer professors are less likely to behave that way."

"With the exception of you?"

As Cosmin laughed, John considered that in his university system, bribing of professors was unheard of. "So have they tried to bribe you?"

"After the regime fell and Ceausescu was killed, I had hoped that would be the end of all of that."

"And my question?" John said.

"Students generally know not to try to offer me money, but a few have."

"And did you purchase anything noteworthy?"

"Don't be absurd," Cosmin said. "Now they avoid offering me anything. But for some other professors, it still persists, no change."

"I don't see much damn change going on," John said, thinking of Alina's situation. "If it's happening at all, little evidence is out there," he added bitterly.

Cosmin stood. "It's true my friend, but let's not consider that now. For tonight, I am optimistic."

"Oh?"

Cosmin strode the room as if he were prowling his lecture floor. "I'm glad you enjoyed my lecture," he repeated. "You have truly inspired me."

"For heaven's sake, I just sat and listened."

Cosmin was now halfway across the room. He suddenly appeared grave, and stared at the floor. "I saw Alina near her office this evening," he said, monotonically.

His abrupt mentioning of Alina surprised John. "I spoke with her recently."

"Yes, I know that," Cosmin said, still gazing at the floor. His voice was subdued. "As I told you, she and I attended University at the same time."

"You did mention that." John wondered how he was privy to his interaction with Alina.

"We were all in love with her, but too intimidated by her," he said. He released a plastic laugh. "It was too much for us to overcome."

Cosmin was moving in a certain direction; he wanted to make a point. "She is formidable," John said.

"But I thought, after all these years, and with my lectures succeeding, why not?"

John looked up from his drink.

Cosmin stepped farther from John. "Why not do what I've been petrified of doing for so many years." His voice gained momentum. "Do what I've lacked the confidence to do. But what you, John, have given me the confidence to believe is finally possible."

"Do what?" John said, dreading the answer.

"Ask her on a date," he declared, his clenched hands before

him. "I believe, at last, it is finally time." His eyes were now fastened on John. "But do you think it the right move?"

The wine tasted like vinegar. Perspiration dotted Cosmin's temples, and a patchwork of stubble decorated his face. He waited, foregoing breathing, for John to speak. His left eye twitched. The wait was too excruciating. "So what do you think?" Cosmin beseeched. "What do you say?"

John's purple wine seemed glutinous now. "You need to do what you feel is right," he said.

Cosmin strode forward, stamping the floor. "Then ask I will," he yelled. "Thank you so much my friend. I've waited forever for this. Tomorrow I'll do it."

"Shall I open that second bottle?" John said.

# Chapter 14

On the way to Casa Alba on Strada Decebal, he considered how many people now inhabited the buildings he passed. These were once grand, single-family homes, constructed in the late 1800's and early 1900's in the Neo-Romanian style. Their facades were decorated with elaborate ornamentation and carvings, often surrounding the windows and doors and rising up the towers, in this architectural style particular to Romania. Carvings of ropes, twisting vines, imperial birds, and perturbed faces with flowing hair were meticulously fashioned in the crenellated walls. Rooms were unabashedly large back then, and had been furnished with sumptuous portraits of august individuals, and mahogany shelves were stacked with heavy leather volumes. Immense fireplaces, crackling with dried pine, warmed the inside and threw shadows across the splendor. But this was not to endure. Post World War II, after the communist takeover, these homes were hacked into numerous tiny apartments with flimsy pipes cursorily installed, the paintings and books were burned for heating, and the structures were neglected and decayed.

Before John was a grand house with a tower on each corner capped by a greenish copper pinnacle. In the twilight they seemed two colossal soldiers who had witnessed over the years, from their lofty position, the seizure and butchering of their home. The maroon tiled roof remained, with more than a few tiles absent, and it angled drastically towards the brittle, frozen lawn. The artwork and treasures once sequestered here had long been pillaged and vanished to parts unknown. In the final shreds of the evening's light, the soldiers seemed slightly hunched, but some luster lingered from the remnants of the once esteemed architecture. It must have been splendid.

Had Cosmin already spoken to Alina today revealing his amorous intentions? John did not know. He'd confirmed their dinner plans, which he had been tempted to retract, with a terse call to Alina that covered only their meeting time. He'd listened for peculiar intonations in her voice but didn't detect any; perhaps Cosmin had not confronted her. Soon he would know. If she were pleased with Cosmin's advances he would be astounded, but he had seen improbable events unfold before.

The early February weather was parsimonious with warmth. A brisk wind began to rise. The cold sun plunged below the hills but the restaurant sign, inscribed in white neon, was clearly visible a half a block ahead. Casa Alba, a hotel and restaurant, had been installed in one of the aforementioned homes, and part of its incongruity was its status as the single place of business in the vicinity.

The entire hotel had been painted white several years ago. After passing through the iron gates and traveling along a cobblestone path, John entered through the double doors. The décor immediately appalled him. Instead of preserving the marvelous dark wooden floors commonplace in the old homes, the new owners believed wall-to-wall cream carpets were more tantalizing. They were dreadfully mistaken. A concierge, whose lips were concealed by a mustache rivaling the carpets in thickness, asked John how he could help. It was not easy for John, but he did refrain from saying by tearing up and burning the rugs, and instead stated he was present to dine.

The dining room was a wide space with high ceilings and chandeliers. The tables, covered with cloths and silver oil lamps, were all unoccupied. The concierge left. A waiter, his head bursting with white hair, reclined in a chair against the white wall and vacuously observed him. A compromising moment ensued: John hesitated to sit without the waiter's approval for fear of offending a sensitive soul, yet the waiter offered no aid. The waiter's hesitation wasn't due to boorishness, but by the shock engendered by the arrival of a patron. Finally rising, he scampered towards John with diminutive but rapid steps, and offered an extravagant bow to allay any discomfort caused by the delay. Although it had the opposite effect, John politely informed him he was expecting a friend, but would sit and read the menu.

The heavy menu had John anticipating an extensive read. Alina appeared before the table. The carpet had muffled her steps. She wore a dark business suit and carried an enormous workbag over her shoulder.

"A pleasant day?" John asked.

"Quite a place," she said, looking around.

John studied her aspect for signs of distress, and was immediately disquieted by her glazed eyes that stared vacantly at the silverware, the lamp, and other arbitrary objects. She was silent. He had not seen her this way before. Cosmin must have already spoken with her; he must have professed his alleged love just a few hours ago. It must have been distressing for her to deal with, regardless of her feelings for him, for they were acquainted for many years and she would want to handle him judiciously. But how had she responded to him?

"How was your day?" John asked.

"You already inquired."

"And I already failed to receive an answer."

Alina wasn't looking at him. Usually she stared at him with raptness.

"Much could have been done with this place," John said. "It's too bad."

"Isn't it?"

Cosmin's affectionate professions had apparently depleted her energy, but John realized, aghast, that her dearth of ardor might apply solely to their present meeting. It occurred to him she might have been pleased with what Cosmin had to say. Although Cosmin was not considered overly handsome, and his character continually lapsed into weakness, maybe she found his feelings endearing. For goodness' sake, maybe she was willing to reciprocate!

"You seem quiet tonight," John said. His phone was vibrating in his pocket. Cosmin was trying to reach him to discuss his experience with Alina.

"Do I?"

"What troubles you?"

Alina's face colored. "This inquisition of yours."

The situation certainly upset her, for she knew that he spent plenty of time with Cosmin, and that he might be aware of what had transpired. "Our definition of 'inquisition' must vary. I'm simply posing rudimentary questions that you are indisposed to answer."

"Was your intention to fight tonight?"

Considering what he had said, he didn't believe he had uttered anything acrimonious; at least not yet. But yes, he desperately wanted her to reveal how she had reacted to Cosmin, and he was unsuccessfully suppressing that desire. "Not that I'm aware of."

"Well, you need to increase your awareness," she said. "For if I am 'troubled', as you insist, then perhaps consideration of that condition would help."

John leaned forward, his elbows on the table. "And thus I have inquired about you in an attempt to offer support for anything that ails you. But I must first identify what ails you in order to do so."

The waiter was on the verge of asking what they would like to order, as his forefinger and eyebrows were raised, but after Alina turned to him and he witnessed her expression, his pallor matched his hair as he backpedaled into the corner.

Alina faced John. "I believe we're all aware of the history of your helping anyone other than yourself. That would make a short volume."

Consternation and then some anger flowed, but he did endeavor to extinguish it. "Perhaps. But you are not supporting my attempt to do otherwise," John said, flipping a fork onto the table. "In fact, you seem quite intent upon preventing me from helping."

She appeared contemptuous. "I question your motivation."

"As well you should. I am attempting to be civil to an unreasonable person."

Alina stood, hurled her bag over her shoulder, and departed.

After a few minutes, the waiter, eyes fastened to the carpet, noiselessly approached. John hoped he would offer him any reason to release his ire, for he would seize the opportunity with vehemence, but the man was keenly aware of this and abstained from smiles or eye contact. He delicately inquired if anything was needed, and John said no, nothing was required.

On the way to his apartment, John didn't bother buttoning his jacket against the glacial air lashing across him. He assessed his magnificent dinner; it had not unfolded quite as planned. Perhaps Alina was partly accountable, for she was clearly troubled from the start. But he also, regardless of the innocuous appearance of his comments, had been afflicted with anxiety, and she likely detected a bit of the animosity he began to feel due to the fact that she would not mention her conversation with Cosmin.

His phone rang again, and it was Cosmin. John turned off the phone.

In his apartment he lay on his bed, attempting to feel one frozen hand with the other, not an efficacious enterprise. The high ceiling was an inky darkness, and he breathed the musty odor. He didn't bother turning on the soba to heat the room.

The next morning, John awoke to the light streaming through his windows, a silver dust drifting listlessly amongst the rays. He thought it to be around eight o'clock. He still wore his clothes from his evening out. After changing and boiling black tea, he turned his phone back on. Moments later, Cosmin rang.

"What is it now?" John demanded. A conversation with Cosmin was not an appealing option.

"I haven't been able to reach you."

John poured the steaming dark tea into a mug. He added a touch of milk.

"Where have you been?" Cosmin said.

"Do you have something worthwhile to say?" The tea thawed John's purpled lips.

"I couldn't," Cosmin said.

"Couldn't what?"

"Tell her. Alina."

John placed the mug beside the sink, spilling some tea onto the counter. "You never spoke with her yesterday?"

"It wasn't right. I wasn't ready. I don't think I'm right for it. "

"So did you speak with her at all yesterday?" John demanded, walking to the window.

"No. I was reluctant to telephone," Cosmin said. "You're the key. You need to give me more encouragement."

John hung up and called Alina; there was no answer. He called her four more times over the next hours, hoping each time if he pressed the phone buttons harder she might answer, but this ingenious technique proved ineffective. He left a message, then left another and waited. It was a struggle, but he waited.

Two days later he spoke to Cosmin, who informed him that he had just discovered through a friend that Alina had resigned from her job on Friday after failing to receive the promotion to vice president. Some guy by the name of Vlad had received the position. John realized this must have occurred only a few hours before they met for their dinner. Cosmin said she left Cluj the next day, moving to Turda, a smaller, troubled city farther south where her father abided. Cosmin stated that he knew all along pursuing her affections was an absurd idea but an amusing one, and he would now abandon all ridiculous thoughts of her. He coughed, and then heartily invited John to join him that evening to visit a purportedly wonderful underground bar.

Whether the moldy pong troubled others he was unsure, but it had no effect on him. In the last three weeks since his unfulfilled dinner with Alina, he had inhabited these underground cave bars so frequently the smell became imperceptible. For initial visitors, the odor narrowed their eyes and prompted slurs, but if they sadly chose to remain, it eventually faded into just another element of the environment. After an even longer duration degenerating below, the drinkers themselves began to acquire a faint tinge of the mold and smoke that they subsequently conveyed throughout the city. A person who regularly inhabited these bars was often detectable by their slovenly appearance, but always by their odor.

Cosmin tilted the dark bottle towards their glasses and poured some foul grain spirit. A slab of cedar that had supplied innumerable feasts to worms functioned as their table. John had not moved for what seemed several hours, but time was difficult to gauge here. Few other visitors were present. Forms withered at the bar, and one other table was occupied. Cosmin announced that as the night arrived, the bar would fill, yet they were far into the night and the population remained sparse. For John, this was of no consequence. He hadn't spoken to anyone, and didn't plan on doing so. He had begun to shun these cavern bars that he had haunted during his first months in the city, he had been drinking less, but after Alina's departure, he now once again found himself submerged inside them.

Alina's passage three weeks ago had not significantly stirred Cosmin. After mentioning it several times in the days immediately afterward, he spoke of her no more. His habits and behavior remained static. He continued lobbying John to join him out in the evenings, and lately John offered little resistance.

John had called Alina numerous times after he learned she had left Cluj for Turda, but never an answer. After five days her phone was shut off. He had not spoken to her since she had stormed out of Casa Alba. It was excruciating to acknowledge, but yes, he had failed her.

John was back underground and any progress he had made was destroyed. The lure of these bars was clear: one didn't have to ponder reality in the dimness, as everything in the world above faded into the surreal, and in these dank realms below it was all burning alcohol and watery stares.

# Chapter 15

As John lay on his bed, several open books resting on their pages beside him, he realized he hadn't visited the Opera in weeks. The cast surely must be wondering if he had abandoned them. It was a legitimate question. He had suddenly stopped attending after Alina's departure. Yet it might be relieving to see them. After some uncanny deliberation, he believed a visit could be managed.

That evening he headed to the theater. It was a Thursday performance, and even fewer souls would be present than on a Friday or Saturday show. When he sat in his usual seat and looked up from his single-page program, members of the orchestra waived at him, a few swinging their bows. They wore expressions of not only delight, but what seemed to be relief as well. The twin violin players motioned for him to approach the pit. He hesitated, jostling in his seat, but his refusal would surely sadden them so he complied. They lowered their instruments, and she vigorously shook his left hand while her brother tended to his right. The other musicians nodded approvingly and broadly smiled.

This contact brightened John, and he took a clear note of this. Seeing and interacting with them was refreshing. He admired them for their talents and dedication to their craft. They, like the cast, received meager payment, but they continued to press on. And they seemed so pleased to see him. Rapid questions began.

Where had he been? Indisposed, but he was glad to be back. How had the shows been, John asked. Not bad, but not at the level they desired, and of course the audiences were lean. John told them he was anticipating a sublime performance.

Minutes before commencement, the young messenger boy who had delivered his note during a previous show undertook the same task. Seeing him was not a complete surprise as John expected some contact from backstage, and he thanked him and slipped him money and the boy dissolved into the side shadows. The note, signed from the "cast", requested his presence during the intermission. Apparently they didn't want to wait until the end of the performance. Of course this perceptive cast had already spotted him; although he had not seen any heads peeking through the curtain, in this theater, as in most, myriad places to observe from existed, perhaps even more from the stage side.

The show was engaging. The orchestra and actors performed well and John lost himself within the intrigues of the initial acts of Tosca. He recognized most of the cast members, including Lavinia as Floria Tosca, and she gave a kinetic performance. But at intermission, he wanted to eschew the backstage visit. Not that he didn't want to see the cast, for he did, but he just wasn't prepared yet to interact with everyone, as presenting a continuous upbeat disposition would necessitate a quality performance of his own. Perhaps if he relaxed outside first he would be more inclined. He swiftly passed through the lobby and breathed the cutting air in front of the theater. There was little movement in the Piata Avram Iancu across the street, and the dark silhouette of the Orthodox

Cathedral loomed in the distance.

"So you are back."

Visual identification would only be gratuitous: it was the theater's director. Tibi's bass voice and dry comment conceded his identity.

"Is that a surprise?" John said, without turning.

"And you are enjoying the show?" he said, in a tone elevated by his appreciation for John's indentifying prowess.

John turned, and scrutinized the tuxedo bursting with his rotundity, and the massive orange tip of his cigar. "Impressive cigar."

The comment pleased Tibi, as he removed it from his mouth and surveyed its mahogany leaves. He pressed it against his nose, nostrils expanding, and his sallow tongue flickered a taste of it. "Cuban of course."

"They are doing a fine job."

"It's the roll. The Cubans know how to properly roll a cigar; it's essential for the pull."

"I was referring to your cast and orchestra."

As Tibi looked at John with momentary discomfort followed by sustained loathing, John detected the sweet odor of brandy through the pungent smoke.

"And, as I have mentioned, they could be doing even better with more support," John said.

Tibi was a man unaccustomed to being challenged, by anyone in any facet of his life, and he had not anticipated John raising the issue again. No one else ever did. Accordingly, he struggled to navigate. "Unfortunately the government doesn't give much," he tried.

"Perhaps not. But what they do give could have a major impact," John said. "If actually applied that is."

Tibi, his countenance momentarily petrified with angst, promptly regained composure by puffing on his cigar, each pull seemingly inflating him.

"And the next show?" John asked.

"Aida," he said, huskily

"I look forward to it," John said, reentering the lobby. Tibi remained behind in the cold, both he and his cigar smoldering.

As John entered the orchestra, the messenger boy, panting, was beside him and passed on another note. It again requested, or perhaps insisted, on John's presence backstage; he was to proceed through the left back hallway. It wasn't signed. John had planned on returning to his seat to review his recent encounter, but the arrival of this solicitous second note persuaded him otherwise.

John had ventured through this backstage path before. He entered the greenish, gently curving hallway, barely lit by a few lanterns fastened to the wall. He waited, breathing the moist, moldy air. Cloth ruffled, and the elaborate base of an expansive dress became visible around the bend before its occupant. Lavinia, her face painted white, appeared wearing a scorned expression accentuated by the dimness.

"Are you avoiding us?" she demanded, her eyes moist.

This dramatic a reception had not been expected. "What's wrong?"

"You received the message before the show. I saw that," she said. "Are you avoiding us?"

She possessed a tortured demeanor. "I was outside. But you already know that."

Her expression didn't change.

"Don't be absurd," John said.

"Are you upset with us?"

"Why do you ask that ridiculous question?"

"You haven't visited in weeks. What is it?"

John stepped closer. "I have been busy with other things," he said, not wanting to discuss his recent tribulation. Calming her was imperative. "I do have other places I need to go, mind you. But, I must mention that I'm enjoying your particular performance tonight."

Shards of pleasure momentarily materialized in her aspect, but she soon grew grave again. "Were you speaking with Tibi?"

"I was." She did not miss much.

"Stay away from him," she warned.

"So Tibi is the callous 'he' you had told me about last time."

"Please stay away from him John; he's known for a barbaric ruthlessness. It's safer to just stay away."

Intermission was ending soon. John complimented her outfit, and watched with fascination as Lavinia peered at her dress through the meager light and looked back at him with radiance and joy. Her emotions had altered drastically enough that he wondered if she mistook their interaction for a pivotal scene from Tosca.

"Maybe you can visit afterwards?"

"Not today, but I will return soon," he said. "And please, will you tell everyone I said hello?"

"That I will, you can be sure."

The lights flickered and she hurried back down the hallway, her dress cockling and ruffling emphatically. John returned to his seat for an enthusiastic second half. At the end, he stood and applauded, waved at the orchestra and cast members, and left the theater as the curtains closed.

The Piata Unirii teemed with the midday crowd. Typically, most didn't stop here since the sites for food or drink were relatively expensive, but this impressive city square was at the crossroads for various neighborhoods and thus hurried pedestrians were plentiful, shuffling through in diagonal paths. The exceptions were those who

chose to relax on the benches curving around the piata and observe
the tumult. These benches surrounded the intimidating statue of
Mathias Rex, who sat garbed in armor triumphantly atop his horse,
his awestruck soldiers looking up to him with admiration. But because of the biting February weather, few embraced the reclining
option, and continued on their way, with Mathias haughtily observing them as they passed.

John watched the people slip by but saw only cocoon-like forms
scuttling, as they remained buried deep within their coats. His
woolen coat and thick scarf offered some respite from the cold.

After the crowds tapered off, John walked along the strada.
He halted upon identifying the prodigious figure of Tibi, standing
with his massive legs saddled apart, talking to someone by a café
door. He had never seen him in the daylight before; an appall-
ing site regardless of the time or illumination. A closer viewing
revealed that the "someone" he spoke with was Patrick. John remained concealed, and Tibi departed momentarily. John entered
the café, filled with the brazen yet enticing odor of burnt coffee. Its
steamed glass front faced the Piata Unirii, and Patrick sat smoking
at a table in the center of this facade.

"So there you are," a delighted Patrick said, extinguishing his
cigarette in the wide ashtray before him.

"Brilliant deduction," John said as he sat at the small, iron
table. So how did Patrick know Tibi? Never had he seen Patrick at
the theater. John ordered a black tea, and leaned back in his seat.

"Your scarf is magnificent," Patrick said.

"How is the University?"

"Not bad," Patrick said. "For the students are sharp. But the
professors don't speak to me, so my time is spent with students or
alone."

"Perhaps your complete ignoring of these professors has
slightly dissuaded them from conversing with you?"

Patrick's eyes narrowed but he smiled. "Honestly, they aren't particularly social. Most are much older and they aren't willing to mix with anyone they haven't known for at least fifty years."

The waiter placed the tea on the table. John added a spot of milk, and Patrick shook his head. "Plain tea is the way."

"That all depends upon the tea." John sipped. It was time. "I noticed you were speaking with that Tibi."

Patrick paused, looking at John with curiosity. "You know him?"

"From the theater."

A man passing on the sidewalk diverted Patrick's attention. "That is a jacket worth seeking." The pedestrian wore a sleek, dark overcoat.

"So how do you know him?" John said.

"I don't."

"You were speaking with him five minutes ago."

Patrick appeared perplexed. "You mean Tibi?"

John nodded.

"Oh, I barely know him. I met him at home in France."

John had been heedful to appear insouciant, but he now realized Patrick was aware that his interest in Tibi was of a higher level than he was displaying. At times Patrick was acutely perceptive. The problem Patrick's discovery posed was that the disparity he detected between John's demeanor, and true desire, would inspire Patrick to add a histrionic element to his answers.

"He comes to Bordeaux a few times a year," Patrick deliberately said. He gauged John's reaction while lighting a cigarette. "He is an acquaintance of an uncle."

Patrick was revealing little, but getting him to divulge, if in fact there was anything interesting to tell, was simply a matter of accusing him of being prosaic in any way. "Sounds mundane," John said, looking aside.

Patrick's muscles tensed with chagrin. "Well, he comes to make bank deposits and investments. My family has been in the banking business for generations," Patrick said, rapidly. He moved to the edge of his seat and looked directly at John. "But it is odd."

"Yes?"

"They call him Tibi here."

"That's odd?"

"The name, not necessarily. But when I met him in France and when he's banking back in France, he used a different name."

"Which is?"

Patrick swirled his wine, contented once again that John hungered for information that he presided over. And oh no, he couldn't just freely give this data out, for that would be utterly plebeian. He gazed at the pedestrians. "Which is what?" he innocently asked.

A bit of hardship was requisite to acquire an answer. "The other name that he uses. What is it?"

"The other name?"

"Yes."

Patrick gently sipped his wine. "Claude."

"Claude," John said, laughing. "A departure from Tibi."

"Who knows? I only met him twice, briefly, at large parties, and my uncle mentioned in passing that Claude lived here in Cluj. And those deposits, he must be involved in all sorts of activities that I'd prefer to remain naive about. But that's how I heard of this place."

John signaled the waiter for a refill.

"In France, with my family and our estate, I have met hundreds of people from around the world."

"And he greeted you upon your arrival here?"

"Greeted me?" Patrick said. "He didn't even know I took a university post here, and I only saw him on the street a few months after I arrived. He didn't recognize me at first, and when I introduced myself he was quite shocked, believe me. But as I said, we don't really know each other, and have not been in contact. And I don't think either of us wants to change that," he said, laughing. Patrick frowned as John added more milk to his tea.

"How were you aware that he's called Tibi here?" John said.

"You're just bursting with questions today," Patrick said, jocularly, but received no reaction except a firm silence. "Someone greeted him while we spoke. He told me that's the name people like to use for him around here."

It was time to change topics. John warmed his fingers on the thick tea mug. "So have you been enjoying yourself at all?" John asked.

Patrick gradually exhaled. The response would not be affirmative.

"I try. It's not easy."

"That is true."

"But anything is better than being proximate to my family, the illustrious oppression troop."

Considering Patrick's inclinations, he must have had to cope with a fair amount of acrimony in the stiff old money society whence he was raised.

John had not shaved in days, and sleep was inconsistent. Patrick scrutinized him. "And you?" he gently asked.

"As long as you refrain from prompting another major altercation, I should be fine."

They both laughed heartily, and Patrick ordered a tea, with "no milk" required.

The railway station was a disappointment. Considering the city's fairly large size, he hoped for a grand building, but the sta-

THE SUNLIGHT LIES BEYOND

tion, located away from the city center, was a two-roomed, rectangular structure with water-stained cement walls. A membrane of dubious characters surrounded and inhabited it, regardless of the hour. These sorts were of no surprise, as most rail stations throughout the world, and irrespective of their architectural grandeur, possessed them.

He passed the station late in the afternoon, while various men with far-reaching mustaches flashed hollow watches and gold-colored metal at him and muttered unintelligible prices. John avoided eye contact and they retracted into the crevices. A block farther along the main Strada Horea were a few narrow grocery stores with prices that varied significantly according to the customer, but that were consistent in their policy of offering no receipts. Employees from the railway station and those who worked or lingered nearby slid into these stores for cigarettes or beer.

Down a side path, beside the tracks, a few coarsely dressed men were lined up before a window. The man in the front, who stomach protruded to a degree that a column would be useful to support it, walked away from the window while plunging his gaping mouth into a hunk of fried dough. These placintas, sold in several locales throughout the city, offered a filling but hardly nutritious mealtime option. Many were filled with salty cheese or blackberry fruit preserve. John had sampled them and could understand their appeal, as they were undeniably tasty.

He joined the line. The dusty ground rendered his formerly black shoes to a pale hue. The man directly in front of him, squat and balding, turned and smiled. A few of his teeth were still intact. He pointed his plump finger at a tall, attractive woman walking down the main street a hundred feet away and he grunted, again revealing his scarcity of teeth. John interpreted the gesture as a sort of bonding attempt, so he nodded. This seemed to satisfy the man, who turned back to the line.

A stout, elderly woman with a gauze eye patch and a white bandana tied over her hair hoarded the customer's coins and doled out the placintas. Despite her size she moved rapidly, with a hardened scowl that intimidated even the men on the line, for they ordered solemnly and lowered their heads while waiting. Directly behind her was the cooking room encased by greasy walls, and a young, slender woman, also wearing a bandana and a stained apron, rolled the dough and dipped the chunks into a cauldron of snapping oil.

The railway tracks were close by, with emaciated clumps of dark Bittercress growing in patches along the iron bars and shards of brown beer bottles strewn about. The man ahead of John mumbled his order, and when the old woman moved away to fetch it, he whistled and clucked at the slender woman working near the cauldron, and veered towards John seeking another nod. John ignored him and the slender woman did not look up. The man, not to be dissuaded, whistled once again and slapped his behind at the woman and turned, smiling at John. The young woman glanced at the man and then at John and she paused, her mouth agape. She whirled away and looked down, slamming her chin into her chest. A sharp streak of recognition shot through John while the old woman berated the customer, who was instantly subdued. John struggled to identify the young woman. Yes, for heaven's sake, he believed he knew who she was: Lavinia. It was difficult to correlate her majestic costumed appearance on the stage to her current position leaning over the steel cauldron in this greasy, feverish back room absorbing derision. But it was she. Her back now faced him, and she wasn't moving. John swiftly departed without ordering.

As he walked down Strada Horea back towards the city center he was dismayed. Hopefully Lavinia did not believe that he'd recognized her, for their eye contact lasted but a brief moment. Most likely though, she knew he did. She was proud of her position as the lead actress at the Opera. When others thought about her, she wanted them recalling her performances on the stage. Of course she did. It was a coveted job that she had earned by her phenomenal voice and her years of dedication to the craft. But her salary was so measly that she must have had no option but to toil in that humid, oily room, covered with that bandana and listening to disparaging remarks. Most people who frequented that placinta pit were hardly opera aficionados, but still, for someone like Lavinia, whose image was essential to her career, that type of exposure, however limited, must be disheartening.

The streets were fairly quiet, for it was a cold Saturday. John increased his pace as he headed back towards the Piata Unirii and his apartment. A snow-haired woman stood outside an apartment building, her fist on her hip, watching a child kick a tattered ball along the sidewalk. She yelled for him to return when he wandered too far. John heard her shouting again after he had passed. The buildings began to transform back into Baroque and Gothic architecture as he neared the city center, but their elegance offered no comfort. He thought of Turda, where Alina had moved over a month ago. What ever had happened to her there? Never had she called. He had heard Turda was an impoverished city, undergoing even more trying times than Cluj. It was dreadful to consider the possibilities, but the chilling thoughts pranced about in his mind.

He surveyed the city from his apartment. It was darker now. When he thrust open the window, frigid air ambushed his room, which wasn't a bastion of warmth to begin with. No cars drove by below. The crows that often perched on roofs across the street were absent. Few signs of life existed. He thought about Alina. He must go to this Turda.

# Chapter 16

Switching gears was not a smooth procedure; the automobile jerked rebelliously with each pull. He had purchased the Dacia, which according to title was nine years old, for a low price, and he had fleetingly experienced the delight one feels when conducting business well, but he now recognized that he might not be on the triumphant side of the transaction.

The car engine wheezed and popped as he climbed Calea Turzii, the road twisting up the hilly southern part of Cluj. A transport truck passed him. He now recalled with dismay the sight of the elderly woman with heavy lipstick whose lips gradually curled upwards, and whose lengthy teeth were thus ominously displayed, as she deftly counted the cash after the car sale.

Fortunately the climb wasn't too steep. The Cluj apartment buildings had tapered off as he ascended, and were gone by the hilltop. He peered over his left shoulder to view the city below, but was greeted by an invidious honk from a car nearly attached to his bumper. The view, a grand one, would have to wait. He began coasting down the hill, slamming the stripped brakes to limited avail on the curves. Calea Turzii, called a highway, had a single-lane on either side, with occasional areas for passing.

To suddenly see open, natural vistas was a relief, as it had been some time since he experienced these types of views. The last buildings he had passed in Cluj were communist-era apartment blocks. Now he faced sloping hills with patches of lofty conifers faintly whitened by the light snow. He had not departed from the city in months and presently experienced the onrush of liberation, which although was somewhat quelled by the intense sputtering and repining of his vehicle, nonetheless persisted.

In time, the land leveled and the snow faded, with expansive fields on both sides of the road. These vast clear spaces, with neat rows of dark humped soil and furrows, were dormant farmland, and he hoped to return in a few months to observe the seas of corn and wheat rustling in the spring winds. An abandoned tractor rusted in the distance.

Ahead was a curious patch of bright blue. As he neared it, and might it be noted his car's laggardly pace did not hasten this advent, it turned out to be a small house with an oaken wagon by its side. What a unique color for a house; the blue glowed as he passed. And its proximity to the road was bewildering, for not more than six feet separated the pavement from the front door.

Testing the limits of his marvelous vehicle didn't seem judicious, so he maintained a moderate speed. Few cars were on the road. Out of habit he checked his fuel level; he was aghast. He leaned forward, squinting to ensure he was reading the gauge correctly: empty. The tank had been full upon purchase, and that was this morning. He had travelled only a few kilometers. How this happened he couldn't say, but his more exigent predicament was the dearth of petrol stations or anything else in the vicinity. The dark fields, with occasional spots of white powder, stretched into the horizon as far as one could see, monopolizing the landscape.

For optimum fuel efficiency, he decreased pressure on the accelerator. Ahead was a vehicle of some sort, but not a car. He neared; it was a wooden wagon replete with piles of shattered tiles and planks. A hooded individual gripped the reins of the horses, their ribs visible against their sides as they labored to pull the load along. John continued driving. Purportedly it was seventy-five kilometers to Turda and he had travelled perhaps twenty.

The car would perish momentarily. Did tow trucks exist along these roads? He tried to will away the passing kilometers, or cajole the fuel tank into ignoring them, but the sight of a cluster of bright blue ahead provided a welcome interruption to this farce. Four houses rested nearly against each other, and John parked beside the first one. After he turned the key to off the car, its entire frame palpitated and then froze, and his belief in it restarting would hardly be deemed unassailable. Outside was silence. No vehicles passed and no one was visible. He wasn't delighted with his pending task, as knocking on doors and requesting petrol was not an appealing endeavor, but without petrol he wouldn't be arriving in Turda, or anywhere else.

All the windows were curtained. He knocked on the doors of each abode, and received the same unwelcoming response of stillness. At the fourth house, after rapping on the door, a banging emerged from inside. This banging, a thrashing of metal, persisted for almost a minute. The door finally opened, exposing a thin, elderly man wearing dark pants, an undershirt, and a feathered cap. He didn't appear surprised or concerned in the least that John stood in his doorway saying nothing, and a few seconds passed, the man remaining phlegmatic, before John realized he was supposed to speak. He recounted his predicament, underscoring that the tank was full just earlier that day, and that he was clueless as to what happened. The man said nothing, then vanished into the house leaving the door ajar. He returned with white slippers but no jacket. Outside, he pushed ahead of John, entered the car, peered at the gas meter, and his body quivered. He was laughing. He stepped out, and the laughter was replaced by a wide grin.

He cradled a piece of clear gum in his palm. He explained to John, rather gently, that the petrol gauge had been manipulated, an old practice mind you, and that the gum had been employed to fasten the needle to the full position. It must have fallen off while he was driving.

John recalled the woman who sold him the car and how she'd emphasized, several times while negotiating the price, that the tank was full.

"Have you any petrol?" John asked.

The man strode to the back of his house without responding. John didn't follow, for his headlong departure intimated that he remain. A metallic scraping resounded against the house wall, and the man returned carrying a sizeable rectangular can, rusted in color. Although thin, his gaunt, muscled arms possessed a wiry strength, and lifted the can with ease. He handed it to John for inspection. From the weight and the slapping of fluid inside, John surmised it was nearly full. After taking back the can, the man poured the contents into the fuel tank of the car. Despite wearing only a sleeveless undershirt, he didn't appear the least bit cold. John wondered why he trusted this man, as he was unsure what was flowing into his vehicle, but in truth he had no choice. He requested twenty lei, a reasonable price for that amount of petrol, if it was in fact petrol, and John paid. He thanked him and the man graciously bowed, lifting his cap. John departed, warily checking his rearview mirror for any celebratory gestures.

After he passed more desolate farmland, it began to drizzle; the temperature was just above that requisite for snow. The sky was gray. He hesitated before turning on the wipers, worried they might not function, but he flipped the switch and following a protracted groan they squeaked and swabbed at least a few of the droplets from the windshield. He rejoiced, for at this point he was not demanding much.

A massive structure skulked in the distance and he knew he was approaching Turda. Closer, he observed it was a factory several hundred feet from the left side of the road. Jutting out of the filthy concrete halls were three smokestacks with blackened peaks. The lot in front of the factory was empty. He passed several similar buildings. All were immense and grimy, and all were quiescent.

The rain fell harder, pounding against the car's thin metal roof as water veins trembled down the side windows. The wipers continued to squeak, moving across the windshield at varying speeds. The first apartment buildings, bland and pallid, appeared on both sides of the road and were not an enticing welcoming sight for the city. Due to the precipitation and the covered sky, it was relatively dark for three in the afternoon. The apartment blocks continued, one building indistinguishable from the next.

It dawned on John, who had once prided himself on his planning proficiency, that he had absolutely no forthcoming strategy. He journeyed here to see Alina, but he didn't know where in the city she was located, and she wasn't privy to his arrival. Of course she wasn't; they hadn't communicated since she departed Cluj a month ago. John considered, appalled, that she might not even be in Turda anymore.

He persisted along the main route through the city, the buildings slick with rain, and reached a small downtown area that was a marked improvement, aesthetically, from the outside areas he had passed. Turn of the century buildings, three or four stories high with ornate facades, lined a wide avenue, and a white Orthodox Church with gracefully curving domes silhouetted against the drab sky. He located a hotel nearby.

Sitting in his narrow room three floors up, with the windowpane reverberating from what had now transformed into sleet, he deliberated how to proceed. He had attempted calling her phone from a payphone, and it rang and he immediately hung up. At least it was working. So was he to phone Alina, say hello, and inform her he happened to be sitting in a hotel room in Turda? Of course, this was predicated upon her answering his call. If she did choose to converse with him, which was improbable since she hadn't contacted him since their dinner debacle, the phone call would not last long. What was needed was a reasonable amount time to communicate with her.

His fingertips pressed against the chilled window as it quivered, and he solemnly observed how the streaming sleet and the gray sky chastened life around him. Hooded and capped figures below moved in a seeming trance: as cars slipped on the roads, splashing sheets of muddied water across them, none of these figures even reacted. The urge arose to flee and return to his apartment in Cluj. Yet he had progressed this far and couldn't conjure any rationalization, despite relentlessly trying, for delaying contact with Alina. He stared at his phone at her number, his thoughts colliding in crashing waves. Finally he dialed, and after three rings she said hello.

"It's John."

Silence followed. "How have you been?" Alina said.

Her voice was clear. "Fine actually. Not bad at all," John said, pacing his room. "And you?"

"Where are you?"

John tensed. "What do you mean?"

"What I asked. Where are you?"

"In Cluj of course," John answered. "And you?"

"Turda, south of Cluj. I've been staying with my father," Alina said. "I've found work directing cashiers at the supermarket."

John didn't respond.

"Still there?" Alina said.

"Absolutely. So you are well?"

"I'm fine."

"Well then, it was nice speaking to you."

Alina said goodbye and John hung up. He stepped back to the window, his fingerprints on the glass. He tossed his phone onto the bed. The call had been useless, and he had been useless. He had his opportunity to speak with her and he accomplished nothing, except of course prevaricating about his whereabouts. Focusing on the sky, he morphed into the dire gray to which he already belonged.

John awoke with a start. All around him was darkness. Unaware of his location, he stared at the murky walls, and after a few moments, the previous twenty-four hours inundated back. Standing at the hotel window, he watched slivers of the morning whiteness rising against Turda's horizon. An icy draft maneuvered through the warped window frame. He retreated to bed. If he was to venture outside, he would at least await the accompaniment of the full morning light, however paltry that companionship may be.

He tightened his scarf while traversing the piata. For the first days of March, it was cold. Through this chill a café emitted the odor of fresh coffee, and John was easily lured inside. The other patrons, embedded in layers of sweaters and jackets, regarded him. These must be the regulars. They stared not with alacrity or hostility, but they just stared, and without embarrassment. When he looked directly back at them, hoping to ward them off, their gazes did not waver in the least. A seat in the back offered a bit of respite from their stares, and eventually, but not immediately, they returned to their smoking and conversations and reading of newspapers.

A plan was needed, however feeble. Speaking with Alina was

crucial, but after his initial disaster, the idea of phoning again was abhorrent. Between sips of bitter tea, he considered visiting the food markets in town. Alina had mentioned she managed one, and he would perhaps encounter her. Yet another illustrious plan, John thought. What in heavens would he say if, by small chance, he did encounter her: "My, what a coincidence!" Though the plan would not garner accolades for perspicacity, it would impel him to traverse the city and possibly meet Alina, so he accepted it for now.

He ignored the narrow stores he passed, searching for a larger market, the type she mentioned she managed. He had reviewed a map of Turda and hence applied some methodology to his search, but after over an hour he had not unearthed a single location that could be considered a "supermarket" by any interpretation of the term. He had descried few stores of any sort, and the city was fairly empty and stationary for a Monday morning. The single store he had entered peddled sodas and candy, and was inhabited by a lone bearded employee grunting fitfully in his sleep behind a cluttered counter.

He persisted through the streets, ignoring everything but the rare storefronts. This restricted observation fastened him to his task and shielded him from most of the general bleakness. There was limited activity and energy all around him, but he wanted to avoid pondering this for the moment. His ears, reddened and beyond feeling, prompted him to consider telephoning Alina and simply stating he was in town and inquiring where she worked, but that course was far too straightforward for his skewed logic to accept. By mid-afternoon, he burned with frustration at the fruitlessness of his search and headed back to the hotel for a hot shower.

Nearing the hotel, he observed several children yelling and dashing down Strada Clinicilor, apparently chasing after something. After pausing, he chose to cross over onto this street for a few minutes more of seeking. About one hundred yards down, he noticed a medium-sized storefront, and the pale green of vegetables was visible through the glass. Several people, carrying small bags, exited. This could be the one. Not a gigantic store, but compared to those he had seen, it might qualify as a supermarket. He was roused but apprehensive, for if Alina was indeed inside, what he would say was still unbeknownst to him. He loosened his scarf and entered. The smell of wet lettuce greeted him. The inside was larger than the front revealed, with six registers and numerous aisles. After the silence of the streets, and the reduced scale of all he had encountered, the activity was surprising, however minor. An office was alongside the registers on the far side of the room.

Realizing he was still planted in the doorway, in full view and inanely staring about, he darted down an aisle. He raised a sack of biscuits, and feigned reading the label while observing the office. In fairness, he was fully aware it was not the most convincing performance. Inside were several figures moving around, but the translucent window on the office door prevented identification. The biscuit bag suddenly popped, so tight was his grip, releasing the odor of stale cookies.

A young man, at most eighteen and slightly shorter than John, stepped boldly to his side and spoke: "Looking for someone?" His hair was closely trimmed on the sides but atop his head it was several inches high, defying the laws of gravity with an unsparing portion of gel. He wore an apron and a nametag that read: "Bogdan".

"Pardon?" John asked.

"You're staring at the people in the front. Maybe I can help you."

The audacity of the comment was astounding, but John was also surprised at the perceptiveness of the speaker. "I was looking at these biscuits."

The young man smiled as he walked away. "If you need to find someone, just ask."

John returned the biscuits and raised another packet to ignore. After several minutes he acknowledged he need no longer foster his current pretense, for the office remained shut and Alina was not at a register, if she happened to work in this store at all. Bogdan stood at the far end of the aisle stacking cans.

"Enjoying your work here?" John asked him.

"So who are you looking for?"

John was momentarily appalled, and then he laughed. While Bogdan's persistence and intrepidness might irk most, John was amused. "I have a friend that might work here."

"Might? Why all the stealth?"

"Enough questions," John said, firmly.

Bogdan instantly straightened in a manner similar to an army cadet, and his aspect transformed into one of compliance.

"Her name is Alina," John said, gently. "I believe she runs the cashier department."

"Alina," Bogdan said, brightening. "She's here. Of course she's here."

John tensed. So he had found her, she was near. "Where?"

"She's in charge, she's usually in the front office you were watching."

John didn't want to knock on the door, as his elaborate planning only reached this juncture. Some time was needed to ruminate what to say so this opportunity wasn't completely razed. "I'll come back another day." He turned to leave.

"Where are you from?" Bogdan said.

John peered back at Bogdan, scanning his eager face. "You have many questions."

Bogdan looked down at the blue and red tomato cans.

"New York."

Bogdan shoved a can across the shelf. "That's fantastic," he exclaimed. His eyes widened and his face flushed. "Fantastic. I've read plenty about New York, and about the U.S. And I plan on visiting the Empire State Building and working in New York."

"Good."

Bogdan chewed on the inside of his mouth. He finally said: "If you want, I actually can show you around Turda a little, only if you want to of course." He clutched a can and waited. "Only if you want to."

John's instinct was to proceed alone, but Bogdan's initial comments and temerarious attitude had impressed him. It was time to move apart from some of his instincts. "You're working tomorrow?"

Bogdan shook his head side to side.

"Tomorrow at nine. In the piata down the street."

"Excellent. I can show you all over the city, I know all the streets. I can show..."

"Just show up," John said, turning to leave.

"Should I tell Alina you were looking for her?"

John faced him and Bogdan stepped back. "No."

"No, of course not. Of course I shouldn't."

"Tomorrow I'll see you," John said. As he slipped out he glanced at the office and detected no movement inside.

As John arrived at the center square at ten minutes until nine, Bogdan paced beside an iron bench. Spotting John approaching, he sat and extended his legs, striving to achieve an aloof pose.

"Ready for your tour?" Bogdan asked. A New York Yankees baseball cap was perched atop his head, and he struck a lighter in vain several times underneath a cigarette.

The left corner of John's mouth arose while watching the failed lighter. "Let's go."

The cold sky was laden with seemingly infinite layers of burdensome clouds. As they walked across the piata, Bogdan straightened his hat. "Your American history, I've read plenty of. I wrote an excellent paper on your Revolutionary War."

"How is school?" John said.

"I'm done."

"With what?"

"School." Bogdan peered at John. "I'm waiting to maybe apply for college."

"Waiting to maybe?"

Bogdan shuffled forward. "I have to get a few things together."

They passed a ghastly modern sculpture comprising vertical steel strips that were incongruous with the old square. The turn of the century buildings around them, although few in number compared to Cluj, were quite handsome, though not extremely well preserved. Bogdan walked backwards, facing John, as he felt a proper tour guide should.

"What we have here is Piata Republicii and some of the architecture," Bogdan said, majestically motioning to the finest buildings. "And here are two churches, both very old. Older than your country in fact." Checking John's expression he discovered only impassivity. "We can look into those and then to the City Hall, which might be similar to New York's but I'm sure not as big, and then we can come back here to the center and some stores."

"Cut the nonsense," John said, rigidly.

"What?"

"You heard me."

Bogdan's mouth was an oval. His backwards walk halted.

"I'm here to see Turda," John said.

"But that's what I was saying," Bogdan said, quickly. "If you prefer we can start with the stores and..."

"Perhaps you didn't hear me. I told you to cut the nonsense."

Bogdan's face reddened. His mouth churned, unable to manufacture words. "I don't need to visit a clothing store and the City Hall," John said.

Bogdan stared at him, but the ability to speak or express himself had departed.

John continued. "We're going to look around, but not just within a few streets of this city center and a couple of stores. I want to see what Turda is really like these days. We'll visit some of those factories I saw when I drove in, some of those large apartment complexes from communist times."

Bogdan shook his head from side to side.

"What is it?" John said.

"Why would you want to see all that?" he asked, clearly perplexed.

"I'm interested."

"You don't want to see all that. It's not a good thing."

"But I do," John said, firmly. "Now if you don't want to go there with me, then that's fair enough."

Bogdan kneaded his chin. "You're a bit strange."

"So what will it be?"

"It's not nice in those places," Bogdan said, pleading. "You don't want to go around there."

"Are you coming or not?"

Bogdan took off his baseball cap and stared at the cobblestones. "Well, if you want."

"I want," John said. "Let's go."

A bus took them to the northern section of the city. The roads were barely paved, as holes occupied more surface area than asphalt. They exited amidst a patch of broken bottles that had been shattered along the sidewalk. A brisk wind was burdened with the smells of sour sewage and burning wood.

"Are you happy now?" Bodgan asked, looking around.

Four-story rectangular apartment blocks occupied both sides of the street. Their facades were simply unpainted concrete, and most entrance doors had long since vanished. Piles of garbage surrounded the overflowing bins, and rustling sounds emerged from deep within these heaps. Although John was intent upon exploring, he harbored no misgivings about keeping the origin of these sounds a mystery. Further north, smokestacks loomed over the apartment buildings.

"Do you know about that?" John asked, pointing to the stacks.

Bogdan stared at them for several moments before responding. "Sticla Turda. A glass factory."

"Is it open?"

"It used to be very busy once."

John glanced at Bogdan.

"Yes," Bogdan added.

John led as they walked towards the factory. Silence predominated, and the potent odor of burning wood persisted. Frayed towels and undershirts hung from windows. A bundled figure passed, coughing violently and spitting onto the ground. The crooked trees alongside the sidewalk were skeletons from the extended winter.

The road transitioned to dirt; crushed stones mixed with the blanched earth. John's legendary automobile would have had no chance traversing these roads. After they passed a final apartment building, the immensity of the factory was fully unveiled. A few cars were parked against its front. Past the factory were empty fields, and farther in the distance were gradual, forested hills.

"So it's still functioning?" John asked, pointing to the factory.

"Is what functioning?"

"Your intellect."

Bogdan looked confusedly at John.

"The factory," John said, smiling. "Is the factory still operational."

Bogdan was relieved. "A part of it."

The iron doors in front were shut. "Can we get inside?"

"But why?"

"I want to see."

Bogdan straightened his back and shoulders; slightly, to be sure, but John noticed. "I actually know them inside," he announced.

As they neared, Bogdan shuffled beside John. They passed through the corrugated fence, mostly still intact, and moved towards the main entrance. The factory consisted of three connected buildings, all an ashen color that melded seamlessly with the bland sky beyond.

"You know," Bogdan said, circumspectly, "they won't want to see you inside."

John paused and looked at Bogdan, who awaited some reaction. They resumed walking, and before the doors Bogdan's hands fidgeted with heightened anxiety.

"We'll just say I'm visiting from the U.S., and I want to see the factory," John said. "Relax." While uttering these words John was in the process of contending with his own uneasiness.

"But why?" Bogdan implored. "Why?"

"I like factories."

The metal doors, decorated with thoroughly rusted hinges, scraped and creaked open. The first room was nearly empty. What might have been a greeting counter beside the door was now an abandoned slab of yellowed plastic. The walls were bare, discounting grooves and discoloration. Resonant clanking sounds, emerging from somewhere distant, seemed subterranean.

"We can go to Mr. Lescu's office," Bogdan said.

Their footsteps echoed in an immense barren hallway. The bases of the windows were fifteen feet above the floor, so although waxen light streamed through high above, only sky was visible. They turned left and passed through another hallway. The clanking grew more immediate.

Bogdan stopped before a door. "John, I'm just asking, but are you sure you know what you're doing?"

"Who is Mr. Lescu?"

"The head engineer. He's in charge here."

"Are they still producing?"

"Not often. They're desperate for any orders, and he'll expect that you have an order for them." Bogdan's eyebrows lifted. "Otherwise, he will be upset."

"Let's go inside."

Bogdan knocked on the door, but no response. He looked at John, and John nodded. After hesitating, he knocked, and a voice barked from inside. The office was sizeable, with a desk near the back wall and two chairs before it. The remainder of the room was only empty space with a high ceiling, and thus the furniture appeared far tinier than it actually was, like well-positioned toys in a dollhouse. Seated behind the desk was a tall man about fifty, with a soot-colored mustache and a solid jaw. He stood. A blue work cloak was buttoned down to his knees. He greeted Bogdan and instructed him to sit. He had not even looked at John. When John and Bogdan both sat, he followed.

"How is your father?" Mr. Lescu asked Bogdan.

"Bored."

Mr. Lescu gently smiled and shook his head. He finally turned to John, staring and saying nothing.

Bogdan interceded immediately: "This is a friend of mine, John, from New York. He's here from New York."

Mr. Lescu surveyed him. "How do you do?"

"Fine. I hope to have a look around your factory."

Mr. Lescu picked up a pen. "You order is for bottles."

"No."

"Then your order is for other glassware of course."

"I would like to look around," John said. "I have no orders."

Mr. Lescu's eyes narrowed and he dropped the pen onto the

blank paper before him. He stood and deliberately stepped to the desk's side. On the wall behind him hung three black and white photographs of the factory from busier times. A photo of younger-appearing Mr. Lescu in the center of a crew of around a hundred workers hung in the middle.

"May I ask you something?" Mr. Lescu said to John.

"Certainly."

Mr. Lescu gazed at the photos on the wall and stroked the thin frame of the central photo. "Are we here for your amusement?"

Bogdan's hands collapsed into his lap.

"I wouldn't think so," John said.

Mr. Lescu moved adjacent to John's chair and glowered at him. "Then what the hell did you come here for?"

John stood directly in front of Mr. Lescu and examined his rugged face. Streaks of gray lined his dark mustache. A moment of severe silence passed. "I'm interested in your factory and the work you do," John said. "I could visit anywhere in Turda but insisted on coming here, and I'll happily return at any time that is more convenient for you. Just instruct me when."

A few inches separated them. Mr. Lescu's eyes didn't waiver from John's. John was static. The clanking sounds persisted some-where beyond the walls.

"Then come with me," Mr. Lescu said, placing a hand on John's shoulder. "Let me show you around so you can see."

Bogdan stroked his forehead with his cupped hand, and he began to breathe again.

They returned to the hallway, with Mr. Lescu beside John, and Bogdan trailing a few steps behind.

"You probably noticed a lot about this place," Mr. Lescu said.

The question was jeopardous. "I haven't seen much yet."

Mr. Lescu's eyes flashed. "Most of the plant is shut down. Only eight percent is still operational. The rest, it is just wasted."

They descended several flights of stairs. The rising clanking and banging, although surely not charming modulations, comforted John, as they intimated that at least some activity was occurring within the facility.

"What do you do in New York?" Mr. Lescu asked.

"I was involved in investments."

Mr. Lescu stared at John, who prepared for another question. None came. They stopped before a door, with Mr. Lescu's hand firm on the doorknob.

"We have an order for bottles from a local beer company," he said.

"Excellent."

Mr. Lescu paused, momentarily looking at John with curiosity. "It would be, but like all of the few orders we receive, it's not much. Let's take a look," he said, opening the door.

An enormous room was revealed, hundreds of feet in every direction, with immense steel conveyors and intricate engines and tanks. Lines of hundreds of windows surrounded the room just below the lofty ceiling, and fluorescent lights dangled over the conveyor belts. Overall, it was an extraordinary sight that required time to assimilate. It was fairly dim, as most of the lights were off, and the windows were oddly situated too high to affect the floor. Bursts of hotness emanated from the few functioning machines in the room's center. Other than those, all machines were dormant. As John surveyed the scene before him, he sensed Mr. Lescu's eyes fastened upon him.

"Let's talk with Ron," Mr. Lescu said.

They crossed the sandy floor and approached one of the functioning conveyors. Two men in dull blue work cloaks were flipping switches and tugging levers. Bogdan had remained behind. Mr. Lescu greeted the proximate worker with a pat on the back and the man bowed. John now remained several feet away, for he thought it best to allow Mr. Lescu to explain this slightly anomalous situation freely. What Mr. Lescu said was not audible, but he spoke fervently with his hands splayed before him. After several nods between the men, he turned and motioned for John.

"This is Ron, in charge of the production floor and the staff here," Mr. Lescu said.

The squat, bearded man with tiny and nimble hands observed John in a remote manner. His eyes were mostly whiteness, as his iris and pupils were uncommonly small. "I am in charge of the entire floor staff," he said. "All six of them." He broke into a sharp, sustained laughter.

John was disinclined to join in on his laughter, due to the joke's ribald and unseemly nature, and of course because it was not funny. As a compromise he briefly smiled, and had little doubt Mr. Lescu continued to intensively study him.

"John's interested in what we do here," Mr. Lescu said, stepping away.

Receiving his cue, Ron explained to John, in an animated fashion, the melting process of the silica, sodium carbonate, and lime, and the tremendous temperatures they heated these elements to. Slightly over nine hundred and eighty degrees Celsius he said, a very uncomfortable temperature no matter the season. Producing glass was nothing new, as glass products had been dated back over five thousand five hundred years ago; older than his wife. Mesopotamia and Egypt were the first regions manufacturing, not quite local areas he emphasized, and so there was a little bit of history behind all of this.

After pointing in seemingly random directions, he told John that the other rooms housed even grander machines that had been inactive for years. He used to direct them all. They were all useless now, as the funds didn't exist to maintain them, but he reemphasized that he used to be in charge of them all and the entire floor staff. Everyone was gone now. Then he stopped speaking. John glanced at an impassive Mr. Lescu. Ron squinted, water swamping his eyes and his lower lip quivering, and it appeared tears were on the verge of falling. John lowered his head, his hands fastened before him, bracing for the scene. Suddenly Ron chortled hysterically. John could not often claim he hadn't even the foggiest clue of what was occurring before him, but that claim could be rightfully made at this moment. He observed Ron with fascination. Mr. Lescu stoically watched from ten feet away. As Ron's laughter, an enervating high-pitched cackling, persisted, suspicions seeped in concerning this man's mental soundness. John could only wait. After the laughter finally tapered, Ron dabbed his eyes with his sleeve and noted that they had actually been busy once, very busy, with all the machines operating, but it was a long time ago. Everyone was gone now.

John rejoined Mr. Lescu and they departed, leaving Ron behind sedately pulling the levers. As Mr. Lescu said nothing, John deemed it prudent to circumvent the topic of Ron.

"So you were doing well here years ago," John said.

"The factory was busy. No one said we were doing well."

John slid his fingertips across the icy steel of an immense engine.

"The communist government built us, and they supplied orders. We were busy," Mr. Lescu said. "But they barely paid us anything."

"I see."

"Now, that regime has been thrown out. But as you see," Mr. Lescu said, gesturing with his hand toward the dormant machinery, "the transition to your economy is not easy. My employees would like to get there: both to work and to be paid decently, but the transition to your economy is not that simple."

"I have seen that."

Mr. Lescu wheeled towards John, pointing his finger accusingly at him. "We had fourteen engineers working here years ago," he said in a raised voice. "Two are left. I'm one of them."

They were positioned beside a door at the far wall. Mr. Lescu, without looking, instantly located the proper key from the dozens on his chain and opened the door. He stepped into the dimness and John followed. As John's eyes adjusted, another cavernous room became apparent. It was chilly. Damp cement odor pervaded the air, and colossal silhouettes of machinery floated around them. The silence was pronounced, and the scratching of their feet against the sandy floor reverberated throughout the space.

"We also have another room similar to this, also wasted, also useless," Mr. Lescu said. "Now have you seen enough?"

After slamming the door, Mr. Lescu nodded towards the stairway where Bogdan had remained. "Bogdan's father was our best."

"Best?"

"Engineer. He was my sharpest, worked here for nineteen years." He looked at John. "But I had no choice, I had to let him go, like all the rest of them."

The wide conveyors beside John were silent. "What do they do now?"

"Do?" Mr. Lescu said. "What can they do?" For the first time, he spoke in a subdued voice. "Like most that I let go, they waste away. They do nothing, maybe a small job here or there." He looked towards Bodgan, and back at John. "Many have perished from the drink."

John slowly exhaled. "It's an impressive place you have here, I must say that," John said. "What you are doing here is impressive."

Mr. Lescu again observed John with curiosity, his eyes narrowing, and then he turned and strode away. They met Bogdan at the base of the stairs, with Mr. Lescu resting his hand on Bogdan's shoulder as they ascended. John was sure to walk slowly behind so they could speak on the way towards the exit.

"You saw what you needed to see?" Mr. Lescu asked John near the front door. He stood proudly, staring directly at John, his solid figure centered in the doorway. Much of the initial austereness had departed from his comportment. John was unsure if he was correctly interpreting, for the emotion was discordant with the stalwart figure, but John tensed as he detected a desperate pleading in Mr. Lescu's gray eyes: they seemed to be trembling. John was unable to speak.

John and Bogdan returned to the path leading back into the city. John moved swiftly, and all the layers of anguish he left behind tightened his stomach. The door was scraping closed, and when John, finally summoning the courage, turned for a last view of Mr. Lescu, he saw only the building's sealed facade.

The cold air smelled of the burning wood.

# Chapter 17

The supermarket was around the corner; it was two minutes until ten in the morning. Bogdan had informed John that Alina would be present at nine, but John wanted to give her a little time to settle in. He was keenly aware he had to produce on this visit, for he could ill afford another remarkable performance like his phone conversation from the hotel.

Lamentably, he soon found himself in the same compromising position as before: lingering at the end of an aisle, scouting the office where Alina worked. At least the biscuit bags before him were familiar. At the far end of the aisle Bogdan appeared, waiving once and acting as if his work immersed him. This farce failed as he glanced at John multiple times and spent an inordinate amount of time rearranging the same two cracker boxes on the shelf.

John prepared to approach and knock on the office door. Perhaps no one had yet noticed him, but there is only so long one can loiter in a store before attracting unflattering attention.

"John?"

He knew her voice. He struggled to turn. Looking over his

shoulder, he saw the pressed white shirt and tag marked "manager". Her exquisite face was in full display due to her tied hair.

"What are you doing here?" Alina asked. She appeared thoroughly baffled.

"I'm picking up some biscuits," he said, holding up a deflated bag, which it should be noted, was the same one he had popped two days previous.

"Really," Alina said, laughing. "What are you doing in Turda?"

"I thought I would come and visit." John delicately returned the bag to the pile. "To see you."

Alina smiled. "That's wonderful. But why didn't you call to tell me?"

"As you well know, calling was never a strength of mine."

She laughed again, but stared at John with a dash of incredulity in her eyes. "I'm not sure how you found me in this store for I don't think this a coincidence, but I won't push my luck with questions." A group was arguing clamorously in the front of the store, something concerning the weight of potatoes. "I have work to do. We can meet later; if you would like to, that is."

"What time do you finish?"

"Six."

"I'll be outside."

He departed, deeply relieved that the Alina he walked away from appeared healthy and pleased to see him. In case she watched, once outside he marched briskly as if a destination waited. A positive, upbeat energy coursed through him.

Yes, she did seem quite pleased to see him. Hurried footsteps slapped the pavement, and Bogdan, covered with his purple store apron, was dashing his way.

"What is it?" John said.

Bogdan leaned over, hands on his thighs, to stabilize his breathing. "So what happened?"

"With what?" John casually asked, an entirely nugatory query, as he was fully aware of what Bodgan desired to know. If anything, he attempted to temper the importance of the interaction in question.

"Just now," Bogdan said, "with Alina."

He must have enjoyed watching them, John thought, but his diligent surveillance had not revealed much. "Don't you worry about that."

"Are you going to meet her?"

As always, Bogdan's temerity was undeniably amusing. "You don't need to worry about that."

"So what happened John?"

John squinted, marveling how Bogdan's hair managed to remain upright throughout the day, no matter the weather or trials he faced. "And why are you so curious?"

Bogdan threw his hands into the air. "Every guy here is interested in her, but of course no one has any chance." His arms were by his sides. "But then you came along."

"Then I came along?"

"Yes."

It was lightly snowing. Soft flakes drifted to the ground.

"All right, Bogdan. Don't you need to get back to work?"

Bogdan could not depart that conveniently, that would be sacrilege. "So how about we meet for another tour around the city?"

"Now hold on," John said. "Did you so soon forget your whining about not wanting to visit the places I want to see?"

"None of that's a problem. We're a good team."

"Oh are we?" John said, with just a touch of cynicism.

Eagerness dominated Bogdan's mien. "Yes."

John surveyed the fervid lad before him and repressed a smile as he shook his head in defeat. "I'll tell you what. In the next few days, I'll contact you. OK?"

Bogdan straightened. "Excellent. That's excellent. I can show you plenty of places, we will..."

"Bogdan."

"See you very soon then."

As John walked away, the snowfall grew denser and melted instantly on his face. He needed to prepare for his evening meeting. To see anything beyond the flakes became difficult.

So the moment had arrived. It was just before six. John had not wanted to appear excessively early due to the cold, and certainly he did not want to be tardy. He had combed his hair back with warm water and had drunk two glasses of wine, the first one for thirst and the second for luck. Plenty of luck was actually needed, so he had one more. He eschewed the sidewalk in front of the supermarket, lest Alina spot him shivering and blowing into his hands, and thus remained across the street to one side. At two minutes past six she exited and searched about. John stepped out of the darkness into the cone of light beneath a streetlamp, and Alina moved quickly towards him.

"Where would you like to go?" John asked.

"My day was fine," Alina responded, with a slight smile.

A moment was required to absorb her trenchant response. "That's an odd name for a cafe."

Her laughter was natural and clear, and he was relieved she appeared in pleasant spirits. Of many things he was unsure: how the disaster with her prior employer in Cluj had affected her, what this last month in this Turda had done to her, and what her opinion on his sudden appearance here was. But for the moment, at least, all seemed well.

She suggested they visit a nearby café owned by a high school friend of hers. Her former high school was located only a kilometer away. They were still near the city center, so buildings had obscure, red tiled roofs that were sleek in the darkness. The aged, winding streets were narrow and undoubtedly held many secrets, both of the charming and the terrifying types.

Passing through a tight alley, John spotted the tiny sign, 'No-apte'. Inside was a warm room smelling of baked bread, and they sat at a table against the back wall. It was a rather pleasant place. Sitting on the clean counter was a medium-sized bronze espresso machine. It had several black handles, and gently curving pipes for releasing steam, and the polished machine was prominently positioned for all to see. One couldn't miss it. The tables and booths were fashioned from wood and were stained a chestnut color. A few tables were occupied, and Alina waved to several people before they sat.

A thin man approached their table from behind the bar. His attempt at a goatee wasn't entirely successful, as it appeared malnourished against his pale skin. He greeted Alina effusively.

"This is my friend John, he's from the United States," Alina said to him.

John stood to shake hands, and the man squeezed firmly. This authoritative handshake led John to suspect he was the owner, and he saw no harm in inquiring. He would appreciate the question either way. "This is your establishment?"

"It is," he said, surveying the vicinity with satisfaction. "One of the few in this city with any clients," he said, laughing.

Alina watched them vigilantly.

"But never enough, so although I'm glad to meet you, I'm also glad to have more customers," he said, winking. He shook John's hand again. "I'm Alex," he said. "If you need a coffee or espresso, we have the city's finest, so just ask." He returned to the bar.

A waitress brought Alina a glass of beer and John a red wine. When John turned back to Alina, her sullen expression startled him.

"How long have you been here, John?" she asked, dryly.

What had prompted this sudden transformation? "Not more than three minutes," he said. "Don't you recall just walking in together?"

"How long in Turda?" she firmly said.

His wry response had been far from efficacious, as was usually the case with Alina. At this juncture, John didn't want to discuss his prior days in Turda: the searching for her, or time with Bogdan. Little could be gained from raising those topics.

"Just a few days," he said. "But you're the expert, so how do you like being in Turda?"

She inspected him. Now of course she was fully cognizant of his attempt to transition the focus of the conversation away from himself, and he could only wait to see if she acquiesced to his wish.

"I've been all right here," Alina said. "And you came here to see me?"

"Yes. I came here to see how you're doing. And after observing that," John said, "I'm here to get you out."

Alina thrust her beer forward, the glass scraping against the wood. Foam spilled over the rim and gently slid, in a spare stream, down the polished side, the bubbles delicately popping. "What does that mean?"

"It was self-explanatory."

Alina looked around at no one in particular. "And why, might I inquire, should I get out of Turda," she said in a mocking tone.

"You don't need me to answer that."

"Please do."

The few groups in the café engaged in quiet conversation. A lanky man entered followed by a similar figure, likely his brother, and they sat beside the door.

"We both know Cluj is a much larger city, with far more of the career opportunities you want," John said. "And that you deserve."

"Why are you telling me this?" Alina responded, her face coloring. "And by the way, what do you know about here?"

"I know enough to know that you need to move on."

Alex, from his position across the room, sniffed discord and was intrigued. He sipped his sixth coffee of the day, never with sugar or cream, and watched. His latest cup was unnecessary, for four or five were more than satisfactory, but he did have the city's finest, mind you.

Alina bit her lower lip. John primed for an impending assault. "And how about you," she said. "Shall we bring up that minor subject? After all your success in New York, making great money, what are you doing now?"

"Enjoying the appeals of Turda."

Alina's laugh carried a derisive timbre. "You're barely doing anything. You gave up. So don't come down here lecturing me," she said. "You're doing nothing."

"I'm here trying to help you," John said. "I don't consider you 'nothing'."

"You gave up," Alina pursued. "Face it." A thin layer of sweat shined on her brow.

"Believe me," John said, "I'm facing many things." He placed his hands on the table. "But actually, I'm desperately trying to succeed."

"At what?" she demanded.

John swirled the wine in his glass. The fluid's top, a pinkish tint, contrasted with its burgundy base. "Escaping desolation."

A coffee grinder scratched and suffered and then began humming. Alina shook her head side to side as she exhaled, and rested her forehead in her hands. The fierceness drained from her aspect as she stared at the table. "At least you once had success," she said. "That I do acknowledge. And that's far more than I can claim."

"I've told you, I was not successful."

The waitress, a young girl, inquired how their drinks were.

John informed her that they were fine, and was not surprised when Alex subjected her to questions upon her return to the bar.

Alina exhaled emphatically. "It's funny John," she said, pausing to collect her thoughts. "Your career led to this emptiness of yours, yet you are insistent that I pursue mine?"

"I believe you still have a chance to handle everything much better than I did. To put aside some defensive pride that you have developed and to balance things," John said. "Fortunately, I can help you do that."

"And you can balance things?" she asked with some incredulity.

"I'm learning."

Alina looked directly at John. "Why are you so concerned with my well being?"

John squeezed his hands together, pressing his fingertips against his knuckles, as he found it difficult to answer. "I can help." It wasn't quite what he wanted to say.

The brothers in the front stood and faced each other with scowls. They hadn't ordered anything, and bickered as they departed. Alina shook her head. "Let's face it. I'm not leaving here." Her expression was firm, but dejected. "You obviously know by now that no one is ready for my success. Those top positions, I was frozen out of them for years." Alina looked at her beer glass for several seconds. "I have had enough."

John waited. "There's nothing to be gained here."

Alina remained focused on the glass.

"You need to go back," John said, softly.

"For what?" she demanded. "I've had enough. I'm here now, and my father is here and aunt is here." Her open hands were before her, palms facing the ceiling. "Why should I go? So I can imitate your thoughtless behavior and leave everyone behind?"

She was striking hard and effectively, but John needed to remain on course, always something easier said than done. "To leave someone behind there has to be a someone," John said. "There was no one left anymore for me to leave."

Alex watched them from the bar. He was a curious man.

"You don't seem to be skilled at forming close relationships," Alina said.

John tasted the slightly metallic wine along his cheeks. "No. And certainly not at keeping them," John said. "I don't see that as your most commendable talent either."

"If I want to, I can have a relationship," she said, gripping her wet glass. The beer foam oozed between her slender fingers.

"Perhaps."

She turned away. "You sound like everyone else here."

"Oh, I have no doubt you have endless suitors, that's obvious enough," John said. "And I understand other ambitions are on your mind. But maybe your relationship skills have dwindled a tad, or perhaps they never quite formed." He realized the latter part of his comment wouldn't be well received.

"Well let's look at you," Alina responded crisply. "There are plenty of women interested, and you have no one."

"Yet I never denied that. I admitted I've kept to myself in a hermetic fashion, and saying I haven't done a good job with others is a bit of an understatement," John said. His foot tapped against the base of the table. "But I can admit it."

Alina stared ahead. "I see no reason to leave Turda."

"You quit on your career," John said. "I can understand what it meant to you."

"Don't act like I had one negative incident and then fled like a sniveling coward," she stated. "Don't try to turn this into that. It has been year after year of frustration and humiliation, and there comes a time when one must say it's enough. And if there were more that could have been done, I would have jumped at the chance." Alina stared at her amber beer, and her jaw muscles pulsed. "I'm here to stay."

"We'll see."

She stood. "I'm working in the morning. I need to go."

"I thought you just said you're here to stay."

"I was referring to..." Alina paused, a wisp of a smile forming within her intense expression.

"I'll meet you tomorrow, after work," John said.

She left the cafe, with half her beer remaining and a pool of amber fluid serving as a moat around the glass. John lifted this glass and drank its contents in one clean pull.

As expected, it didn't take long for Alex to arrive. His goatee appeared even sparser.

"So where in the States are you from?" Alex said, his left hand tautly gripping Alina's vacant chair.

It wasn't a terrible attempt at casually opening a conversation: just a good, solid question. "You can sit," John said. "No need to prolong the inevitable."

Alex sat, slightly abashed. "How's Alina? I haven't had a chance to speak with her in a few days."

John looked directly at him, and Alex sustained his virtuous expression. His throat quivered momentarily as he swallowed.

"What you really want to know is what we just talked about," John said.

Alex unveiled a wonderful display of abhorrence. His eyebrows drew close together, and he pushed back into his chair. "Not at all," he said. "That's your business. I wouldn't ask about that. All of that is your business."

Alex's expression admirably remained intact, despite the effort required to uphold such a preposterous countenance. "Worry not Alex. I understand you're a curious sort. Relax."

Alex didn't respond; he contended with emotions, none of them tranquil.

"I've known many curious people, so relax."

Alex's lips pursed and nose twitched as he toiled to make sense of the situation and form a suitable response, but John quickly intervened. "So for how long have you owned this place?"

Alex's contorted face calmed. John had offered him a change of direction, and for this Alex appeared relieved, even grateful. "Three years. So far, it's been all right," he said.

"Good to hear."

"I opened it."

"Excellent."

"Don't get me wrong," Alex said. "Thing's aren't outstanding, but times are tough everywhere." His posture straightened as he lit a cigarette; his poise had returned. "Fortunately my family owns the building you see, so rent, it is not an issue."

"Wonderful," John said. What he desired to know was what Alex and his friends thought of Alina, and how they treated her, for this would reveal much. Alex's perspective on Alina's abrupt arrival in Turda would be illuminating. Of course Alex would inevitably repeat, or more precisely, offer a glorified rehashing of whatever they discussed to others, so tact was requisite. But Alex seemed primed to talk. "So how is it having Alina back in town?"

"Obviously we were happy to see her. My wife and I both grew up with her," Alex said. He hesitated. "But I admit I was surprised she returned."

"Oh?"

"Well, Cluj has more opportunities suitable for Alina. It's a much larger place, with more investment opportunities there."

John appreciated Alex's quandary: Alex, although attempting to explicate Alina's situation, did not want to disparage his home city in the process. Turda was where he had always lived, and was where he owned his business and property.

"Now don't misunderstand me," Alex said, deftly exhaling a

thin line of smoke above him. "Cluj has problems too, like all the cities in the country. We've all been trying to recover." He tapped his ashes into a tray. "You've been to Cluj of course."

"I'm spending some time there."

"Probably compared to places you've been, it's not that exciting. I've seen your American cities on the television shows and what's happening there. My God," he said smiling and shaking his head. "My wife loves those shows."

The impressions these shows gave bothered John, they worried him. He didn't analyze why, it was nothing moral, but he had a subtle, uneasy feeling. Which shows they were he was unsure, but he was sure the impressions they imparted were far from veracious.

"But relatively, Cluj is one of the best cities in this country. If anywhere, a possible rebirth would start there," Alex said. He paused, and receiving no response, continued. "So it was peculiar to see her return here," he said. "But this is not that bad a place," he hastily added.

"So why did she return?" John asked. He needed to explore what Alex knew, but had to tread gingerly.

Creases spread around the corners of Alex's eyes. "You probably know better than I." He had spoken freely, but wanted John to toil a little for all this information. After all, there is always some dignity to be maintained.

"I don't think everything with her career worked out," John offered.

As anticipated, no more was required to propel Alex back to his talkative state. "You're right. People have a hard time dealing with her. It's a shame, it really is. Way back in high school she ran everything. I recall Alina devised the plan to finance the theater program we had. I was in a few of those plays, although I wasn't very good," Alex said laughing. "I know she was tops in her university in Cluj as well. It's a shame, it really is."

"It is." John found Alex's progressive attitude relieving after all he had encountered.

"Don't get me wrong," Alex added, quickly. "I'm glad to have her back here in Turda. We have troubles here, but everywhere has troubles. One day it will get better, I hope."

A man with a heavy mustache and a thick coat saluted Alex from across the room, exiting with the stocky woman he had been sitting with. As Alex leaned forward and jerked his seat closer to John, it scratched abrasively against the plank floor. They were beside each other. His fingertips rubbed the sides of his mouth, foraging for his exiguous facial hair. "But at the same time," Alex said in a confidential tone, "if you ask me, Alina would have been better off married."

"Oh?"

Alex's head was askew. "I married when I was twenty. My wife, she was the same age. Most of our classmates married in the same proximity. Like our parents did. All of us did that," he said, his eyes protruding. "So why didn't she as well?" he continued, his voice intensifying. "Why, is it so wrong what we did? Is it?"

A moment of silence passed. Alex's arms were extended and cigarette ashes gently drifted onto the floor.

He suddenly shrunk back into his seat. "But it's her choice of course," he added in a subdued voice, glancing at John.

"Of course," John said.

# Chapter 18

Something was distinct about the breeze. John was unsure what this variable was, why it felt peculiar against his skin, but as it continued to softly gust from over the hills of dark pines he identified the mysterious component: warmth. This warmth was relative, for on a summer day it would be branded a chilly draft, but he closed his eyes and relaxed and let the wind soothe his face.

Earlier in the day he had walked down Avram Iancu and Strada Andrei Muresanu. He was not meeting Alina until six, so he had the day to wander. He discovered a quiet, narrow park ladened with tall, thick oaks and tiny paths. While relishing the warmer air, John was inspired to examine the trees around him, and his research was remunerated by the discovery of a few pale green buds from the first emerging leaves. He crossed the gravel patch to a brown lawn. New grass had not yet surfaced.

Although he looked forward to seeing Alina in a few hours, preparation was essential since their last meeting ended with some distress. An elderly woman with steel gray hair wandered through the park, seemingly in no hurry. She wore an attractive pair of smooth black gloves, and adjusted them several times. Through the lattice of branches above, the sky was light blue, with strokes of white clouds to the north. The sunlight shown in spotty patches, and John stretched his legs amidst an area of brightness.

Footsteps mashing gravel resounded as three young men dashed down the path kicking a soccer ball. Their energy and zeal contrasted starkly with the placid park, and they dribbled and passed the ball and gladly ridiculed each other for even the slightest technical error. As they ran by, John noticed Bogdan was amongst the three. He wore worn black shoes and oversized sweat pants and his baseball cap; perhaps the hair was limp today. Bogdan, ever observant, noticed John a moment later.

"What are you doing here?" Bogdan yelled, astonished. The ball rolled through his legs.

His two friends and John erupted in laughter, and Bogdan, momentarily cross, was a good sport and united with them in humor. He instructed his friends he would join them in a minute. Correctly interpreting this as a request that they depart, they continued dribbling down the path.

"No work today?"

"Not until tomorrow," Bogdan said. "Today only sports. Preparation for the season."

His friends halted one hundred feet away, footing the ball back and forth.

"Have you see Alina?" Bogdan said.

"How many days a week are you working?"

"Between four and seven. It depends. I prefer the four," he said, "But it's up to the store anyway; it's not my choice."

His friends yelled while kicking the ball.

"You played in school?"

Bogdan's hand clenched. "Oh yes. Senior year I was captain. On days off I still try to play." He looked towards the trees before them. "Better than stocking food boxes."

"That's not your favorite place."

"What can I say?" Bogdan shrugged. "I'm sure there are more exciting places."

John nodded.

"I'm supposed to get a promotion in the next months. We'll see," Bogdan said. He peered at his friends, studying them for several moments, and turned back to John. "I've been reading a book about the debates that went on while writing your U. S. Constitution."

"Are you?"

"I've actually got a good amount of history books; I like government structures and their laws," Bogdan said. "Many are my father's, and some I found here and there." He paused. "You can borrow any, if you'd like," he added lightly.

"That's kind of you," John said. "Fiction is what I've been reading these days, and some history as well. You know, it's odd, but back in college I was required to take a few history courses, no choice, and I considered it a waste of effort, but now I actually hunger to read those books."

Bogdan's stepped forward, confident with his opportunity. "I have plenty of books. You're more than welcome to visit and borrow them. Not all are U.S. history, but some are."

"So what's next?"

Bogdan appeared befuddled. "Next?"

"You finished high school."

"Yes," Bogdan said. His tone was blithe, yet he peered at John with circumspection.

"And college? Apparently you have some interest in learning."

Bogdan's right foot tapped the shaded gravel. Cheering emerged from one of his friends as he kicked the ball over his shoulder and back to his front.

"I have to get a few things together," Bogdan said.

"Yes, you fed me that same line before," John said. "Like what?"

Bogdan looked up. His jaw was firmly set. "Things. What do you want from me?"

"An answer to my question, perhaps."

"I don't know."

"Bogdan, one thing I can never accuse you of is hesitating when asking me questions about any of my business," John said. "So why the sudden fragileness when I ask about yours?"

"I don't know," Bogdan said, desperately. "What do you want?" His palms slapped against his sweatpants.

"All right, all right. Let's forget it," John said. He did wonder what immersed secrets fueled Bodgan's impassioned reaction, but pitied the distressed figure standing tautly before him. He pointed to Bogdan's friends. "So who's the top?"

Bogdan was momentarily silent. "Top?"

"The most skilled player."

"Why do you ask?" Bogdan said, softly.

"Like you, I'm curious."

Bogdan still needed a moment to compose himself. He was ashamed of his previous reaction, that was not what he wanted to show John, and it weighed on him. That was not what he was about. "I am," he answered. "They're both not bad, not at all, though overall I'm considered the best. The top."

"You better go teach them how to play."

Bogdan stared at John. "So where do you want to visit today?"

"Not today," he said. "Anyway, you've got your football to practice."

"That's no problem, those guys I see all the time. We can go anywhere you want to see, and absolutely no whining from me, guaranteed."

John laughed. "Another day. Just make sure you play well,

don't embarrass me."

"No chance of that."

Bogdan was reluctant to leave. He hesitated, but ultimately jogged off, joining his friends. John stood and watched the trio running through the park.

◯ ◯

Alina didn't hesitate suggesting a destination. "Would you like to meet my father?"

This was unforeseen. Not only had they yet to greet each other, but he had expected her to propose a location where they could privately converse, or perhaps argue. Bringing him inside of her home to meet family was not what he anticipated. She hadn't spoken of her family much. Her mother had passed away while she was young, and of her father he knew little.

"Why not?"

They walked, taciturn. He deliberated what had incited this invitation. Had she assigned her father to probe him, to judge him? He would just have to see. He commented on the slightly warmer air, and how it was a relief that the days were extending; there was still strands of light even though it was past six o'clock. Alina watched the sky with a contented face and seemed appreciative of his observations. They arrived at a three-floor apartment building surrounded by a narrow lawn and entered through a side door.

John experienced a slight uneasiness as they ascended the stairs. Nothing overly serious, but the feeling was present. "Is there something I should know before meeting him?"

Alina continued climbing. "Such as?"

"Such as whether he loathes foreigners, or any other trite details of a similar nature."

Alina laughed, assuring him it would fine. The apartment was on the top floor. She mentioned that her aunt, who occupied an apartment at the opposite end of the hallway, visited her father once or twice a day.

"I'm glad to hear they get along well."

Alina turned. "Who said they get along?"

The front door opened into a fairly large dining room, with a kitchen to the side, and a television and bookshelves and faded upholstered chairs were positioned in the dining room's corner. It was a bit larger than many of the local apartments. The rooms were well maintained and organized. Alina pointed out her bedroom and bathroom, and her father's bedroom and his study.

"Is he home?" John said.

She didn't bother knocking when opening his study door. John was astounded at the number of books piled on the tables, the desk, and even the floor. Reading their spines, he noted many were botanical volumes. Pencil sketches of grasses and flowers hung on the walls, and actual wheat and flower samples were framed under glass. The room smelled faintly like a forest floor in autumn. Alina called for her father, and he stepped out from behind a citadel of books.

"Did you want to see this *Rosa banksiae*?" he asked.

He had a thick, full head of gray hair and lengthy thin nose. One of the lenses of his reading glasses was slightly cracked.

"I brought my friend over," Alina said. "John."

"Oh yes, of course, very good," her father said. He stepped out from behind the books. John was unsure which was more wrinkled, his skin or his clothes. He was fairly tall, John's height, and wore a worn v-neck sweater over a white shirt and cranberry tie.

"Hello," John said, shaking his hand.

"Please call me Sorin," he said. He glanced at Alina. "You can leave John with me now. Fear not, for I can show him many interesting things."

"I'm sure. Just don't show him interesting ways to quench his thirst," Alina said, turning to leave. Sorin turned to John, a vague smile in place.

She left the door open a slice. John had expected the three of them to converse for at least a few minutes to warm the conversation, but she had abandoned ship. He wanted this conversation to proceed well yet this was a foreboding start. Awkwardness ensued, as Sorin silently studied the photos on a book's page. John refrained from interrupting, and from posing a hackneyed "what are you reading?" question, but standing mutely before him was nonetheless disquieting.

"Do you love plants John?" Sorin said. He still focused on the page.

John considered the question. He had been anticipating the spring, the blooming foliage. The question, though, had been powerfully worded. "I appreciate plants, although I certainly haven't studied them a great deal."

"Come this way."

Behind the rampart of books, low lamps illuminated a white table covered with samples of various parts of herbaceous plants: numerous dried grasses, stems, leaves, and spreading roots. Beside these were lines of illustriously colored flower petals, with stigma, stamen, and ovary samples. Cardboard sheets, two well-oiled microscopes, a tin of pins, and several beakers of chloroform were on the left side of the table. A label-free bottle of clear fluid rested near the corner. John had a distinct suspicion concerning the contents of the bottle; he had a good sense for those things.

"That's not solely for preserving the plants, although that's what I try to convince Alina," Sorin said.

He must have seen me staring at it, John thought, impressed. Sorin shut the door, filled two glasses from the aforementioned bottle, clinked them together, and held one out to John. Time was not wasted here. As John examined the fluid by holding it against the light, noting its pale violet hue, Sorin swallowed his. His suspicion was confirmed with a sniff: palinca. His eyes dampened from the pong, and he cringed recalling its exorbitant alcohol content.

"So what fruit was used to make this?" John asked, raising the glass.

The question clearly delighted Sorin. "Palinca has endless options, and not just fruit. Would you believe some even ferment it from horse manure?" His eyes glistened while tracking John's rising eyebrows. "But do relax," he said, his hand on John's arm. "For the horses are distant. This is from *Prunus domestica*, the common European plum, and the foremost fruit for palinca." He observed John's full glass. "You are from the United States, no?"

John nodded.

"Your most common plum is *Prunus salicina*, or Japanese plum,'" Sorin said. "It's quite delicious as well. It was introduced into your country around 1870, and has a more pointed apex and lighter colors than *Prunus domestica*."

John bore the wrath of this fermented form of *Prunus domestica*, and though it was indeed a struggle, he retained a placid front after imbibing. The fresh smell of the grass and leaves and flowers instantly intensified.

"You must understand John, *Kingdom Plantae* is extraordinary diverse," Sorin said, motioning around the room. "Over three hundred thousand species, with more discovered each day."

John observed a cluster of white mushrooms directly below one of the lamps, and detected the aromatic odor of ether. "Few realize," Sorin said, "but fungi are not plants." He looked at John with affection. "Fungi are not photosynthetic. Their food is obtained from surrounding materials, by breaking them down. In that way, fungi are closer to animals. Closer to us," he said.

"For how long have you been researching plants?"

Sorin poured refills, the neck of the bottle clinking sharply against the glasses. "My whole life," he said. "This is what I do."

"Well it seems you certainly know your subject matter."

Sorin shook his head, if not a tad morosely. John reviewed his comment, but couldn't find anything inappropriate.

"You must understand John," he said exhaling. "I was an agricultural engineer for the state for many years. Of course, our purpose was limited solely to maximizing crop yields, so our fields of study were restricted. They didn't want us learning too much, oh no." He rearranged a purple flower petal under focused light. "No, they wouldn't permit that. My real research all these years has been on my own, in private. Few know about it."

Their second palincas had a stunted lifespan.

"Are you cultivating plants anymore?" John asked.

Sorin removed his eyeglasses and tossed them onto the table. As they skittered across the surface, John cringed.

"How wonderful you should ask. I am, at the community garden. My patch is reserved, and in the next days it begins."

"Sounds lovely."

Sorin smiled magnificently. "It is, John. Mind you, you never know what's happening there with some of the other gardeners. Some of them hold this hellish belief that they command the whole property. Ernesto carries himself like he's baron of the land, although the fool has always hinted at Marxist sympathies." Sorin said. "And, his garden yields the tiniest peppers every year."

John nodded.

"Look John, most people have forgotten that plants keep us alive, and that is a travesty. And let us not forget that this lovely drink is provided by them as well." As he handed John a half glass, he added dryly: "Now whether we benefit plants merits a slightly variant answer." He emptied his glass, and John, knowing he had no choice nor minding that fact, exhaled and did the same.

Placing the empty glass upon the table, he detected the sweet odor of pine resin.

When they entered the dining room, dinner was on the table. Bowls of bountiful vegetable soup steamed, and a silver tray of baked sausages awaited them. An opened bottle of Merlot rested in the center.

Alina surveyed John and her father. "I see wine won't be necessary with dinner."

"Now don't say that," her father replied. "There is always a need for wine."

Dinner unfolded in a whimsical fashion. Sorin primarily talked, and as he poured the wine, liberally, he spoke of how the phylloxera plague destroyed most of Romania's vineyards in the late 1800's, and most of Europe's for that matter. He noted, looking pointedly at John, that this destruction was imported from North America. These decimated plants were replaced by grafting cuttings onto resistant rootstocks from North American vines, primarily *Vitis aestivalis*, that had a natural resistance. He then touched on weather predictions for the spring, his strategies for his plants in the communal garden, and praised John's wealth of knowledge about plants, a wealth John didn't believe he possessed. Alina exchanged a glance of mirth with John. Overall it was a pleasant time; everyone was well fed and warmed and in good spirits. At the conclusion of the meal, Sorin excused himself and departed for bed.

"He's fond of you," Alina said.

"I enjoyed speaking with him. And this gardening season, he's excited about the opening."

"That's trouble."

"Trouble?"

"This might be hard to fathom, but it's warfare," she said. She released a terse laugh. "A bunch of them have been gardening in the same plot for years, in constant competition over boundaries and who grows the most productive plants. I've heard about what's going on: sabotaging, screaming, and even a few cases of physical attacks with gardening tools. It's warfare."

John squeezed his chin.

Alina leaned forward. "And trust me, he'll expound about everyone else acting unreasonably, but he's just as bad."

"And now what do they do?" John demanded. "Do they even speak with one another anymore?"

Alina stacked plates. "Oh, they all share a drink together every evening."

John helped Alina bring the plates and utensils into the kitchen. He contemplated Sorin's study and his research. "It's a shame there's no botany department at a university here."

"He would have made a great professor," Alina said, intuiting John's thoughts. "But he had to remain here for the government. And now, it's too late."

"So he had to remain here back then?"

"There were no other options."

John collected the empty wine glasses from the table. "Well we're lucky that times have changed."

Alina glanced at John.

"Come on, why don't we go for a walk," he said, looking at Alina. "And might I mention you're a far better cook than your grandmother."

# Chapter 19

As John entered, Alex wrapped his arms around him and squeezed. He had already hugged Alina. This buoyant a display was unexpected; enthusiasm was definitely not lacking. His goatee though had not been liberated from its drought.

They arrived at eight o'clock, the actual starting time for the party. When Alina had invited him, John experienced a wave of concern. The party would offer a rare and marvelous opportunity to spend time with Alina as she interacted with those she grew up with, and to see how they treated her. He wanted to be sure to observe lucidly and handle her friends diplomatically. These are not always life's simplest tasks. An immense gathering it wasn't; rather, a few couples meeting in Alex's apartment to share some food and wine. Alex's café was in the same building on the ground floor. He lived on the first floor, and a few of his elderly relatives occupied the second.

The lengthy dining room table was covered with an extraordinary number of trays of sliced pale cheese. Beside them lingered a single bowl of walnuts. John, still in the front hall, handed over a bottle of wine that Alex effusively thanked him for. Two young boys dashed in simultaneously from the kitchen and surrounded John by methodically hopping around him. Alex mentioned they were his sons as he walked away. These identical twins with bowl-cut brown hair weren't the least bit shy of John. Alina was already in the kitchen chatting with guests, but when John started in that direction the twins had other plans. They yelped in despair, and upon turning back to them, the slightly shorter one asked that a story be told, and he was startlingly composed while making this request. John hesitated, then entertained them with a few brief tales he had acquired over the years. They listened unwaveringly.

"They like your stories."

A slender woman observed John interacting with the twins through squinted eyes, and as he turned back to check them, both awaited more narrative with mouths slightly agape.

"Kati, Alex's wife," she said. She was slim with short brown hair, attractive, but as she neared him he observed her penchant for makeup, particularly foundation. A lot of these foreign products and brands were just entering the country and were difficult to find; she undoubtedly had located some and wantonly displayed the fruits of her quest. Not wanting her to notice him examining her face, although he suspected she already did, he toiled to maintain eye contact. This was not easy.

As she led John away by hand into the kitchen, the twins howled in protest, but one hissing burst from their mother silenced them. In the rear of the kitchen Alina chatted with another woman, and Alex struggled animatedly to open a wine bottle. Shards of purple cork were scattered on the counter before him. They entered the living room, and in the back was a couple he hadn't met. John remained in the doorway, a few feet away, waiting for Kati to make the introductions. His wait would persist, for instead, she began arguing with them. The three bickered in torn sentences about an issue involving a contract and payments. A departure to the kitchen was tempting, but he wanted to leave Alina free to converse with her friend, so he approached Kati. She and the couple ceased snapping and looked up at him, startled.

"These must be your friends?" John said.

Kati's pupils were dilated as she introduced the couple beside her. Lia was short with a ruddy complexion. Whether this facial coloring was due to her arguing or a fondness for rouge he was uncertain, but either way it was unbecoming. She possessed a box-like figure, solid with right angles. The dark roots of her long blond hair were on display.

"John, we've heard all about you. This is my husband Robert," Lia said.

Robert extended his hand to shake. John could not isolate what was unusual, until he realized Robert was so short and his arm so lengthy; the arm appeared to belong to someone twice his size. John reciprocated with a shake, spending more time staring at the outlandish arm than at Robert's convivial face. Lia mentioned just how much the twins enjoyed John's stories. Apparently those few minor anecdotes were under closer surveillance than he realized. Kati unobtrusively left the room.

"You must tell our children your stories some time too," Lia said.

"All of them would love it," Robert said.

"How many kids do you have?"

Lia and Robert pressed their shoulders together and looked at each other with affection.

"Three," Lia said, still focused on Robert. "And rumor has it a fourth is on the way."

John was about to congratulate them, when both Lia and Robert slammed their index fingers against their lips.

"Shhh!" she said. "It's still a secret."

"Of course," John said, glancing at the others in the kitchen, wondering why he was made privy to this confidential information.

On the other side of the living room John surveyed the snacks. The walnuts and sea of white cheese were a curious culinary offering he had never encountered before, and he was not ruing that fact. Yet perhaps the cheese is of alternative varieties and just appears an insipid wasteland, John considered. He sampled several pieces from different regions of the table, but they were identical: without distinct flavor, more like congealed milk.

"Do you like the cheese?" Robert inquired as he approached, looking spasmodically back and forth from John to the table.

John surveyed the plateau of whiteness. "There's certainly plenty."

Robert beamed. "I thought you would like it. I helped make it in my uncle's village in the countryside."

"You must enjoy producing it."

More people entered, and Alex placed wine bottles in a diamond formation at the table's center. He sat, and everyone followed, assembling around the lengthy table. The plan was apparently to congregate around the cheese for a time. Another couple, whom John understood were friends of Kati's visiting from the south, sat across from him, but no introductions were made. Alina was to his right, and beside her were Lia and Robert. To John's left were Kati and Alex.

Alex stood and held his glass aloft. "To John," he said. "Thanks for visiting our home."

Glasses converged proximate to John's eyes, and he randomly clinked as many as possible.

"You should have seen John with your twins," Lia announced to Kati.

"Oh I saw," Kati said. "He's a natural."

Everyone began conversing.

John leaned over to Alina. "They're making quite a fuss over a few minor anecdotes I briefly related to the kids."

"That's not surprising."

John was on the verge of inquiring what she meant, when he felt a hand on his shoulder. Kati stared at him, and once again he endeavored to maintain eye contact.

"So where did you meet Alina?" she asked.

"In Cluj."

A smile spread, and her left eyebrow lifted. "Well I guess the big Cluj mission didn't work out very well for her, now did it?"

John fixated on the wide grin across Kati's face as she turned away. He was bothered; he interpreted the comment as degrading, and was unaware what had provoked it. Yet was this interpretation correct? An unbiased perspective needed to be maintained, but he needed to probe further.

"I understand that you, Alex, and Alina all grew up together," John said to Kati.

She turned back to him. "Absolutely. And as you see I'm stuck with Alex now," she said, laughing.

Alex smiled at John. "It must be awful for her."

John returned his attentions to Alina. She checked if he was having an enjoyable time, and he informed her it was more accurately described as fascinating. Kati's hand was fastened to John's shoulder once again, but he took the time to sip from his glass before turning to her.

"Lia and Robert went to school with us also," Kati said.

"So we have a reunion here tonight."

"Hardly," Alex said, leaning in. "Reunion is an event, but this is something we do once a week, as we always have. It is our tradition."

Robert stood, his metal chair scraping the floor beneath him, and he stretched his long arm and tapped a knife on his depleted wine glass. The clanging instantly quieted the room. "It's great to be here tonight," Robert said, coughing. "And it's great to have an important announcement."

Everyone was still. "I have the honor of allowing John to make this announcement for us," Robert said. He placed his hands on Lia's shoulders, and they looked expectantly at him.

All heads turned to John. He hadn't the faintest clue of what they were speaking of, but looking at Robert and Lia solicitously gazing at him, he then realized this must concern Lia's pregnancy. For some obscure reason they wanted him to announce it. Everyone continued to stare, waiting.

"I think you're best suited to announce it," John said to Robert.

The sweat beads festooning Robert's forehead momentarily burned under the overhead light. His protracted arm still held his glass aloft. "Don't be shy, John," he bellowed. "Just tell them all."

Alina was looking at John curiously and he decided it was wiser to finish this promptly than to create an extended scene by resisting. "Robert and Lia just informed me they are expecting a child," he stated evenly.

A car honked on the street outside. Alex congratulated them, and then, simultaneously, everyone joined in. Oddly, no one asked any questions. Amidst the felicitations Alina leaned towards John.

"So they informed you when we came in," she said.

"Strangely, I was to be the harbinger," John said. "I do feel so fortunate."

Alina softly laughed. "Haven't you noticed something?"

John turned to Alina.

"When I'm around, marriage and kids tend to be the topic of discussion," Alina said.

John recounted the last half an hour. "And why is that?"

"Because I'm not and I don't have any."

He ruminated over Alina's theory while surveying the chattering around him. Reviewing the previous comments between him and the others, he noted that yes, she was accurate about the primary topics, but he longed to believe that this was all harmless, just the random subject of the moment.

Lia leaned forward onto the table, swinging a knife, and everyone instantly silenced. "Most importantly, we want to reserve John, right now, to be the first person to tell our child stories. We don't want that talent of his to just go to waste," she said, cuing the group's unified laughter.

The wine in John's mouth suddenly tasted acrid. It was clear now, excruciatingly clear; they had all been working in a synchronized operation since he entered the party. Even the young twins had been recruited as part of this. The reason no one appeared genuinely surprised by his announcement moments ago was simple: they already knew. It was a seamless, concerted effort, and he had been their pawn. John was unaccustomed to being fooled, and certainly not to this degree. And if this was everyone's method of tormenting Alina, he would not permit it. Intervention was behooved, but to do so tactfully would be far from elementary, for the rhythm of the party was already in motion. John, a new guest, was bound by certain codes of behavior. He could not just commence smacking heads with the back of his hand, albeit a tempting response this was. Astoundingly, despite the group's iniquitous intentions and efforts, Alina still seemed in positive spirits, laughing and conversing with Robert and Lia. She was impressive, to say the least.

"Do you like theater, Kati?" John inquired.

"Of course. Theater, movies, I like them all. Your American movies too."

"I heard in high school, it was Alina who raised all the money so you could have your theater productions."

The plaster on her face seemed to crumble, but she recovered with a crooked smile. "Some she raised, I think," she said, curtly.

"All the money she raised, I heard."

"Well it's too bad she couldn't have the same success in Cluj."

"She had plenty of success in Cluj," John said. "They were just too insecure to promote her to even higher levels than she reached."

Kati glared at him, festering. "Whatever the reason, now she's back here with us." Alex listened closely.

John experienced a rush of anger. He stood and tapped his empty wine glass with his fork. Everyone fell silent, staring apprehensively, waiting for him to speak. Alex watched, eyes wide. As they all waited, little did they know that John had yet to concoct anything to announce. "To Alina, our brilliant mind," John said. "Here's to her future career success, which, as everyone knows, will be golden."

Fragments of clapping ensued, mostly from Alex and the couple across the table. Lia and Kati placed their hands together two or three times while staring at their laps.

"Let's hope she will be blessed with a family as well," Lia soon injected, ostensibly to her husband, but loud enough for all to hear.

Alina seemed oblivious to the comments. She swirled her wine and leaned on the table, chatting sanguinely with the couple across from her. By now, conversations had resumed.

"Who knows, maybe she actually will have a family one day," Lia said, her statement entwined with a derisive cackle. Any last shreds of tact were waning. She was staring at John. Apparently Lia and Kati were taking turns blitzing, and they could not abandon the subject, so lusting their thirsts were for malevolence. Robert and Lia looked at him, mouths slightly open, bracing for a retort, and he eagerly accepted this challenge.

"If she finds the right person and situation, maybe so," John said to Lia. "But for now, let's hope she gets what the children of this country desperately need her to attain so finally they have a good female role model: career success."

Robert glanced anxiously at his wife's steaming physiognomy; retaliation was imperative or he would suffer dearly later that night at home, or at least suffer more than he normally did. "As you see John," Robert said, "Career success is elusive. Look what happened with Alina in Cluj." Lia continued to monitor him. "But family success is stable, and we are grateful for that." Seeing no modification of his wife's expression, he persisted. "Hopefully one day our dear friend Alina will be fortunate, like my wife." He peeked at his wife for approval, and she placed her hand atop his.

"Well said," Kati said from behind John.

She had been listening to everything; not a surprise.

"I couldn't agree more," she continued. "Our twins are our joy."

"Absolutely," Alex said.

Alina still spoke pleasantly with the couple across the table. The fray seemed to be between John and everyone else. Alina wasn't participating. Perhaps she was just too acclimated to them to bother, or perhaps none of this even distressed her. It vexed John though — he would crush it.

"Your twins are wonderful," John said to Kati. "When I told them the stories, they were quite astute."

"Thank you John. Thank you very much."

"They are bright," Lia confirmed from down the table.

"Certainly, as clever and bright as we all agree they are," John said, "they also, following Alina's path, shall not waste that intelligence away, but rather harness it to achieve in the workplace and help country and society."

Kati was petrified, unable to respond, for she didn't want to repudiate John's compliment, yet lauding the benefits of career was not a viable option at the moment. Lia was also mute, fermenting into a higher proof of bitterness, and mind you she began at a potent level. John seized this splendid juncture to switch topics.

"So exactly how do they make this sublime food?" John asked, holding up a limp slice of cheese.

In the front hallway, Alina stepped towards him. Everyone else was in the other rooms. Clearly, she was perturbed. "What did you think you were doing in there?"

"I was attempting to enjoy the cheese," John said.

"It's time to base yourself in reality."

John shifted his weight. "You're right," he said. "There's absolutely no way to enjoy that cheese."

Alina didn't respond. John placed his hand on her tight shoulder. "I'm not going to passively sit and watch while they're trying to be cruel to you."

She turned away. "They can't help it," she said in a pitying tone.

John waited until she looked at him again. "Neither can I." He checked if their interaction was drawing attention, but thankfully everyone was occupied chatting in the dining room or cleaning glass and silverware in the kitchen. Alex, visible through the doorway, glanced up at John, but instantly looked back down when their eyes met.

"We'll discuss all this later," John said, softly.

Alina smiled faintly. "Thanks for your concern John, really. And you're wonderfully adept at combating their group effort; you know I admire your talent. But as I said, I'm here to stay now." She walked into the kitchen and started laughing with Kati as they scrubbed dishes. Her acquiescent attitude towards them was bewildering, but as he pondered, he realized she had become so habituated to their behavior over the years that she found it more efficient to completely ignore any vitriol. And thus she kept them as acquaintances, and still had invitations and people to spend time with. She certainly didn't concede in the same manner for most of her work colleagues or those in her field from back in Cluj. In fact, as John had seen, and as Alina had acknowledged, her behavior was normally the antithesis of this, but for this tiny group from her youth this was her way. It was a remarkably disciplined approach.

In the living room, Robert and Alex greeted John with a raised bottle of palinca. Robert rocked the grass-colored bottle like a pendulum beside Alex's face. He poured three brimming shots that they lifted and drained.

"It's nice to get a little break from the women, eh?" Robert said, slamming his glass onto the table while focused on John.

Robert was frantically attempting to present himself as an entirely different entity than the pernicious marionette of Lia's he was several minutes ago. Now he wanted to be considered a maverick and expunge the last hour from John's mind. He continued staring, desperately seeking any sign of approbation for his declaration, and for his new façade. It would have been effortless to humiliate him for this ludicrous farce, and it would be deceitful to state the temptation to do so wasn't alive and stirring, but John simply nodded. This salved Robert, who maladroitly saluted with his empty glass. During the entire episode, Alex had gazed somberly at John.

"This new palinca, you have more, don't you?" Alex asked Robert.

"Of course. I told you I brought a bunch of bottles from the countryside."

"I think we could use some more of that," Alex said.

Robert hesitated and peeked at John. "You want me to run and get another bottle?"

"*Do* I?" Alex exclaimed. "You, Robert, are in possession of the finest palinca produced in years, and you're bothering to ask me that?"

Robert hustled away, a contented smile ensconced within his expression.

Alex now avoided looking at John. "So are you enjoying yourself tonight?" he finally asked.

"Thank you for inviting me."

Alex sat at the empty dining table. Burgundy veins formed an emaciated web over his eyes. He requested John's presence.

"You seem to care about Alina," Alex said.

John didn't respond.

"I've received information," Alex said. His vigilant tone evinced that this data, whatever it may be, was being unveiled with hardship. The best course, John considered, was to present a neutral front, devoid of obstacles.

"I see."

"In the next few weeks, in Cluj," Alex said, gaining vigor, "a large closed-ended investment company will be set up."

"Where did you hear this?"

"I know people."

"And who is setting up this company?" John said, permitting the previous question to remain unanswered.

"A small group of private investors. Some from Bucharest, mostly from Cluj."

John slid his thumb across the coarse tablecloth, squishing into the occasional dampness of a brick-colored wine stain. "Why are you telling me about this?"

"Why not?"

"The question is not 'why not'. You're taking the time to report this to me, there must be a reason."

Alex laughed. "I've admired you since I've met you, John."

"I don't see anything I've done worthy of admiration."

Alex shook his head. "Come on, John. We both know what happened here tonight. You defended Alina, and did it deftly. You did it without ruining my gathering."

"You weren't much help."

Alex's head whirled as if he had been emphatically slapped. He stood and stalked away, eventually looking back. "What would you have me do?" he implored, his palms on full display.

John serenely observed his angst. "You still haven't told me why you are informing me about this new investment company."

"Why?" Alex said, exasperatedly. "Why? Because a head financial analyst is needed to run it."

"And?"

Alex was back beside John. Still overwrought, he glanced twice at the door before speaking in a low, subdued voice. "We both know Alina would be perfect. She's the best there is. Not only would she lead that company to success, but it would make her career."

John leaned back in his chair. "I fully concur. But as you can see, my dearest Alex, Alina is not the problem. It's the old-fashioned mentality: they're threatened by her. They won't hire her for that level position and then take orders from her."

Alex sat again and sighed, looking at the auburn rug beneath his polished black shoes. "True. Sad, but true." He clenched his hand. "But now is the time for a move John, and you might have some connections in Cluj that could help."

John shook his head. "No. I have been lying low in Cluj, and my connections are limited to nonexistent." He peered at the dismayed Alex. "Since you're privy to this company, might you know someone?"

"I wish," Alex said, palms before him again. "I just have a few general gossip leaks in the business world. That, admittedly, is the extent of my connections."

Laughter and the sharp clacking of stacking plates reverberated from the kitchen. John considered admonishing Alex for his earlier behavior at the gathering, but chose to let it rest. It was strenuous enough for him to covertly impart this information, yet his reasons for doing so were nebulous.

"And why are you suddenly trying to help?" John asked.

The question breathed life back into Alex. He stretched his right leg, and staidly weighed his answer. "I'm not a mean-spirited person John. Everyone is jealous to a degree," he said, looking towards the ceiling, "but not all of us are dominated by it."

"I appreciate your trying," John said. "Thank you for that."

Alex turned away, touched by John's acknowledgement. John wanted this evening to end in an affirmative manner. "You must come and visit me some time in Cluj."

"I will. I would like that."

"And you must promise me something," John said.

"Of course."

"You will promise to do this for me?"

"Of course, John. What is it?"

"Shave that horrific, wretched attempt at a goatee."

Alex was stunned, petrified in incredulity, but he proceeded to laugh as he probed, with limited success of course, for facial hair with his thumb and index finger.

"By the way," John said. "Do you really consider this palinca you sent Robert to fetch anything special?"

He peered at John, twinkling mischievously. "Of course not."

"I'll tell you what," John said. "I'll get tickets to the opera, down the street from my apartment in Cluj. You can bring Kati, and we'll all attend one night."

They stood, Alex proudly, and prepared to enter the kitchen.

"Funny though," Alex said.

"What's that?"

"I heard the guy running the Cluj Opera is one of the prime shareholders in that new company I told you about. His name I forgot."

John halted. He envisioned himself during the intermission, before the Opera building and beneath the dark canopy of the night's sky, and the immense figure silently smoking a cigar alongside the entrance. The pungent, coarse tobacco odor was penetrating. "Tibi?"

"Tibi, yes, that's it." Alex said. "You know him?"

"No," John quickly said. "Just heard his name mentioned somewhere."

Robert exploded into the room, his flesh ruddy from the cold. He was all zeal, which contrasted conspicuously with the delicate climate. He extolled the benefits of his palinca, and as he poured he listed more of its fine attributes. John was not registering. His mind was elsewhere.

He wanted to say goodbye to Bogdan. Bogdan anticipated more days spent together exploring Turda, but these expectations would not be fulfilled. John was departing for Cluj in a few hours.

Inside the store, which was fairly busy, John was surprised that he noticed Bogdan before being spotted. Bogdan missed little, especially within the aisles of this store. He was scrambling to corral cans that had tumbled onto the aisle floor, and John, prior to addressing him, drew nearer.

"Enjoying yourself?"

Bogdan looked up, startled, and brightened instantly. "I

wondered when you were coming," he said. "I've found the perfect place to take you. Tomorrow I'm off work; there are the old salt mines we can visit."

"Unfortunately, I can't."

Bogdan stood. His purple apron was tied tightly around his waist. "Don't worry," he said, firmly. "I know someone who will let us in. I told you before I can take you places. And it's decrepit; you'll like it."

John gently smiled. "I'm leaving."

Bogdan's aspect was even more youthful than usual. With his doleful expression and erected hair, he seemed barely of high school age.

"I'm off to Cluj this afternoon."

"But why?"

John couldn't prevent laughing. "Bogdan, my apartment is there. Here was just a visit."

"But we have plenty to see."

Two elderly women, grasping each other for balance, slowly creaked by.

"We do. Maybe one day we'll see some of those things. But I'm glad for the time we had."

"And with Alina?" Bogdan asked, motioning towards the storefront. "What happened?"

"Nothing, Bogdan."

The answer confounded him. "I can't believe that."

"You'll need to if you want to believe the truth."

The shock was soon diffused by melancholy. Bogdan focused on the scattered cans of tomatoes on the floor and tapped one with his worn black sneaker. It rolled haphazardly and with a repeated clanging, as the can was warped. "I'm playing some football with my friends this Saturday," he said. "I was going to invite you."

"You'll play well I'm sure."

Bogdan continued fumbling his feet about. "You should stay a while."

"I can't."

He crouched to the floor and commenced stacking the cans. He placed them, one by one, in neat rows upon the lowest shelf. He wasn't looking at John. "You were right," he said.

"About?"

"I was just lazy. About college."

John watched him deftly stack the cans.

"Maybe I'll get some things together and send out some applications." One of the cans clanged back onto the floor and rolled tortuously down the aisle. "Maybe for Bucharest or for Cluj."

It wasn't the most persuasive speech. But then John had never conjectured that Bogdan's ailment was lethargy, for he was energetic and diligent with all other activities he engaged himself in. More was involved, something John was overlooking, for each time the subject of college had been raised, Bogdan had transformed into a remarkably prickly creature. "I'm glad to hear it," John said. "You'll do extremely well."

Bogdan held the blue tomato can inches before his face. "Do you think I want to be stuck with this all my life?"

"Those are actually fairly decent tomatoes."

Bogdan smiled slightly, and John patted him on the shoulder. "Thank you for all of your help," John said, as he walked away.

John travelled towards the front of the store. As he passed the canned olives and asparagus, he heard a child, who had just dashed by him, gleefully celebrating. Turning, he saw the young woman, who also had just passed, alongside Bogdan. She was kissing him. She held an infant in her arm. Her medium length, dark hair hung at the sides of her pleasant, childlike face and she wore a pink sweatshirt with cartoons of dancing sheep. The older child, a young boy perhaps aged three, laughed and tugged at Bogdan's leg. John hastily looked away as Bogdan was turning towards him.

Good heavens: Bogdan had a wife and children. Or at least he had a girlfriend and children. He hadn't even suspected for a moment. It had never crossed his mind. Yet it elucidated much, including his tribulations with the prospect of college.

He wanted to look back again, but continued walking, as Bogdan clearly didn't want him to partake of this information. So Bogdan would not leave Turda. How could he? John felt coarse at making suggestions to him without having grasped the entire situation. In fairness, Bogdan had been particularly assiduous about revealing nothing. The harsh feeling persisted though.

He neared the front of the store, a safe distance from Bogdan. The storefront, entirely glass, allowed the outside light to illuminate the registers. Three registers were open with several customers in each line. He was eager to meet Alina. They had not spoken much at the party the prior evening, and Alina had uttered a monotone goodnight to John while encircled by others, and she left escorted by Lia and Robert.

She emerged from the front office, gripping a clipboard. John made himself conspicuous, if also not a tad imbecilic, by planting himself a few feet away from the office door, waiting for her to notice him. Fortunately, she soon did.

As she approached, with her purple manager's jacket and with her hair tied tightly back, he was astounded once again by her extraordinarily immense and gentle eyes. Their aqua color seemed to pulse. John was too absorbed within them to hear what emerged from her moving lips.

"You should have said you were stopping by," Alina repeated.

John grounded himself by peering at the shoppers hunched over their carts. "Of course," he said. "But I didn't have much time. I'm leaving for Cluj."

Alina's clipboard collapsed to her side. "When?"

"Now," John said. "I wanted to see you, and to say goodbye."

Alina shook her head side to side. She took a few steps away towards the front windows. "I suppose I shouldn't be surprised," she said. "It's all my fault. I wasn't the greatest host."

"I enjoyed my time here with you."

"May we go outside?" Alina asked. She placed her board in her office and briefly instructed an employee standing by a register.

Although cloudy, a few errant sunrays highlighted portions of the smooth cobblestone street. They distanced themselves from the storefront and entered a moist, narrow alley.

She turned to John. "Thank you for coming here to Turda," she said, her voice slightly quivering. "You were most kind."

John's throat tightened. He had not foreseen her emotions. "I wanted to see you."

"I never mentioned something when you arrived, but I had been hoping you would contact me."

John searched for something to say, but was having trouble locating that something.

"Forgive me for being unfriendly," she said.

"You were friendly," John said. "We're both just facing complex times."

"I'll be fine here," Alina said, stroking the sleeve of her jacket. "I have work, and we'll see what happens."

John placed a hand on her sleeve. "It's arduous. You know, I've discovered that people, regardless of their country of origin, tend to lack sympathy for suffering when it is imbedded in an intricate situation. But this is probably due to an inability to grasp and comprehend the situation, more than any innate hardness."

They gazed at each other, then hugged. Alina began turning away, but looked back.

"John."

He stared at her, waiting.

"You're different than other people I've met," she said.

"Well," he said, "we might be able to find a few positive things about me also."

"I mean that positively," she said as they smiled concurrently. She held his hand in the softness of hers. "And thank you for attempting to help me. Please, please don't think I don't appreciate that." Her voice was dry and intense. "I do John. I do."

"I hope we speak again soon," John said, toiling to stay composed.

"I hope so." She faced the ground, closed her eyes, and hurried away. John hovered in the silent alley. Pale moss coated the aged stone buildings. He remained. After an indeterminate amount of time trickled past, he stepped back onto the streets and marched to his car. The smell of dampness from the alley lingered.

# Chapter 20

He was grateful his car had made it this far, for at several junctions during the return drive the intense sputtering and invective hurling of the engine caused him to gravely doubt whether his arrival in Cluj would occur that day. At least he had filled the fuel tank himself. The sight of Cluj below evoked some relief. Incipient leaves decorated the trees along the roads and in the yards and parks. Although they had just begun to emerge, as he coasted down the Calea Turzii he noted that the variance in scenery from the time of his departure was considerable.

Cosmin and Patrick needed to be contacted. Cosmin would be indignant about his disappearance as he would interpret it as a shunning of himself, but this could be readily diffused. John's apartment welcomed him back with a mild musty slap. After opening rickety windows, he prepared a black tea and began to read.

The next day bore a clear sky, and John strode briskly towards the University. Lunchtime was approaching, so pedestrians began to mill about the city center. John passed the City Hall, its lengthy yellow walls effectively reflecting the sunlight. After turning down

Strada Clinicilor, he ascended the path into the campus. Cosmin's classroom was located near the top, and he planned on visiting and perhaps even catching a bit of his lecture.

Groups of students, perched on the stairs outside the faculty buildings, enjoyed the weather. The elms that lined the path were still bare, but would bloom in a few weeks. John entered the cool gray entrance of the history faculty and climbed the wide staircase to the second story. Through the tiny doorway window he saw Cosmin prancing about the lecture floor, his blue tie contrasting pointedly with his white shirt, while students, filling most of the amphitheatre-style classroom, listened attentively. He could not hear through the door, and Cosmin was a puppet, floating and swooping across the floor while gesticulating dramatically for his audience.

John smoothly opened the door and slipped inside, sitting on the first seat in the top row. This stealthy entrance was in vain, for ineluctably, Cosmin noticed him. Cosmin remained composed, continuing to lecture, and he peered up at John several times, although not necessarily with fondness.

The lecture ended after several minutes and the students filed out in high spirits. Cosmin waited on the lecture floor, not acknowledging John, shuffling the same stack of papers repeatedly. John descended to the first row. Cosmin, upon growing fatigued of attempting to straighten the straightened papers, finally looked up. "So where the hell were you hiding?"

John laughed; a charming greeting it was. "On a trip, visiting places in Romania." Cosmin's expression remained distorted, although his curiosity was instantly piqued. "I think you would agree, it's important for one to see a country and learn about its history," John added. This axiom was fashioned to quell further antagonism from Cosmin, and it proved successful. Churlishness drained away.

"Times here have not been bad," Cosmin said, strolling away.

"Oh?" John sensed he harbored news he was eager to impart.

"You should see whom I have met."

"Whom?"

Cosmin placed his stacked papers onto the white lecture table. "A woman of outstanding attractiveness. And, she is a professor here as well."

"When you say 'met', do you mean you shook her hand at a faculty gathering?"

Cosmin tossed a pen at him, and it rattled onto the floor beneath John. "Not at all. I'm referring to social encounters. Anca is her name. Three dates we've been on, and I believe I'm smitten."

John stepped onto the lecture platform and circled Cosmin, who remained smiling with satisfaction. "I'm away for a bit and you are already smitten." He stopped before him. "But does she share any of your emotions?"

"Certainly," Cosmin said, with volume appropriate for his lectures. He patted his tie.

"And these feelings she allegedly is also experiencing, they were engendered by you, or by another?"

Cosmin cringed. "What would you expect?"

"Let me refrain from answering that."

Their interaction pleased Cosmin. He was energized and primed for conversation. He began to randomly sketch on a paper with a long, sharpened pencil. "So where did your travels take thou?"

"Through the countryside," John said, casually.

"Cities?"

"I spent a bit of time in Turda. And surrounding areas."

Cosmin's pencil halted. "Turda? Why the hell would you go there?"

"Why not?" John wanted to evade the topic of Alina with him.

"I could mention two dozen destinations more pleasant."

"Seeking pleasantness isn't always my primary motivation," John said. "For instance, I'm here visiting you."

Cosmin shook his head, smiling. As John was about to dispense the introductory words of a fresh topic, Cosmin interjected. "And Alina?" he asked stiltedly, focusing on John. "Did you see her?"

Cosmin awaited his answer.

"I did."

"Well, what did she look like?"

"She was approximately two-and-a-half feet tall, and was sporting multiple heads."

Cosmin squinted in bemusement.

"What do you think she looked like, you imbecile? Moving to another city doesn't typically prompt a physical metamorphosis," John said.

Cosmin turned towards the immense chalkboard and began erasing with slow, measured strokes. He looked back rather meekly. "Did she ask about me?"

"Why would she do that?"

"She knows you and I know each other."

John surveyed the empty folding seats; the classroom was silent. "No, sorry, she didn't."

From the grooves plowing across Cosmin's forehead, John induced he wrestled with his forthcoming utterance.

"Should I contact her?" Cosmin finally said.

"Why ask me?"

Cosmin paced the floor, gripping the eraser with hands clasped behind his back and gazing at his black leather shoes. "The problem is the same, besides the fact that she has moved, of course," he said. He peeked at John, but was rapidly back to his shoes. "I'm not sure of the best strategy to ask her out on a date."

This took a moment to ingest. And to process. "Ask her out on a date?" John exclaimed. "What are you even talking about? What happened to the marvelous Anca and your dates, and being smitten?"

Cosmin's eyes lowered. "Well yes, of course. She is wonderful. But let's not jump to any conclusions."

"The only conclusion I could jump to is the soundness of your idiocy."

"All right," Cosmin laughed. "But can I help it? If you care deeply for someone, how can you suppress that?"

John moved closer to Cosmin, closing the gap. He noticed two tiny grease stains on the base of his tie. "And this enormous care of yours was so clearly manifested when Alina left Cluj after her problems at work, and you never even once checked if she was all right, or bothered to mention her again," John said. "That was a monumental display of care and compassion."

Cosmin warily watched John.

"Be serious," John said. "You're mistaking a childish infatuation for care."

Cosmin was discomposed, unable to conjure a rejoinder. He appeared as if he would gladly welcome a new course of discussion. "Well, Anca isn't bad at all."

"I'm sure she's not."

John strolled across the creaking wooden floor to one of the windows, which ran from knee level to nearly the top of the lofty ceiling. The afternoon crowd frenetically bustled across the campus. "How have things been here at the University?"

Cosmin sighed, and joined him at the window. An older man whose silver hair reclined underneath a feathered cap, grasped a stack of teetering folders, and dropped one onto the path. White papers scattered across the lawn. As he scurried about, crushing the papers as he seized them, bystanders became involved in the endeavor.

"Not much has really changed," Cosmin said. "I do believe my students are improving; the essence is there. But the negative aspects, the corruption, that's intact."

Outside, the paper retrieval mission had been completed. The owner of the citadel of paper balls effusively thanked those around him.

"I must declare that your students certainly seemed satisfied."

Cosmin turned to John, his skull an incandescent orb. "Let's celebrate," he declared, in a tone suggesting this were a novel idea.

"Oh heavens. It never requires much with you, does it?"

"I know a bar."

"I would have never guessed."

"Well?"

"Not now, I'm busy," John said, firmly. "But we'll be in contact."

John stood alongside his bedroom room window half an hour before departing for the theater that evening. His hand pressed against the thick, cool wall. Strips of deep orange and scarlet plastered the skyline as the sun plunged. The time had finally come. He was ready and he had made the preparations. Patrick would be meeting him in the front. And of course Tibi would be present, as he always prowled the theater during shows. John had to make this work; this was the chance. He had journeyed a long way. But this night, if he miscalculated or handled things errantly, he knew the consequences would be dire.

Patrick hugged John when they met outside of the theater. The hug lasted far longer than John felt was warranted but he displayed no distress.

The evening was crisp, and dusk had nearly transformed into darkness. "It's so good to see you," Patrick said. He wore a navy suit jacket adorned with gold buttons and had a red silk ascot primped below his chin. When John had invited him that morning to a performance of La Traviata, he immediately accepted.

"You know, I was supposed to meet with a friend this evening," Patrick said, with his back to the theater's façade. He bore an enthralled aspect.

"And I'm classified as an enemy?"

"I have a new friend," he said.

"That's a surprise."

Patrick's eyebrows were lofty. "Meaning?"

"If I do recall accurately, you oft bemoaned the dearth of, how did you say, 'quality company', available to you."

Patrick looked across the avenue. The streetlamps surrounding the Piata Avram Iancu were clicking and snapping on. "Yes, well, it's always been a struggle in my life locating suitable company."

John was partially successful suppressing a laugh.

"But," Patrick added quickly, "I have come into contact lately with a few people that aren't wholly unbearable."

"I'm sure they would be ebullient at the level of your flattery," John said, as Patrick looked away again, checking his slicked back hair. "And why didn't you fulfill your encounter with your friend this evening?"

"Certainly," Patrick said, with his hand raised before him, "I could not lose this wonderful opportunity with you." He stroked his ascot. "A friend purchased this in Rome and mailed it recently." He peered back up at John. "I must confess, I was surprised you invited me here to the Opera. This is a first."

John didn't respond. In the distance the luminous columned domes of the Orthodox Cathedral were beacons against a darkened sky.

"Have you been away?"

"Yes," John said. Patrick wouldn't inquire further, for generally he was far too involved in his own affairs to probe into another's, that is unless their affairs directly affected him. But now that John had returned to Cluj, and Patrick could readily access him, the tale of John's travels was inconsequential. From his invigorated manner of speaking and the deeper color to his complexion, Patrick presented himself as more robust figure than when John had last seen him, and he suspected the new friendship that Patrick repeatedly alluded to was the derivation of this alteration. Interrogation was gratuitous though, for if Patrick wanted to divulge information he eventually would, as John merely had to ignore casual references concerning the aforementioned subject, until Patrick could resist no longer and would proclaim his thoughts.

The show wouldn't commence for fifteen minutes, and he had not seen Tibi, but John suggested they sit. So far John was performing fairly well; he retained a placid front and was thinking clearly. The orchestra members would undoubtedly notice him, and he needed time to interact with them. Walking down the center aisle toward his usual row, it occurred to him that this was the first time he attended this theater accompanied.

The sounds of string instruments floated throughout the hall; sounds that helped sooth his tensed nerves. Several musicians had already sighted him and appeared delighted. He instructed Patrick that they would reconvene at their seats. Patrick was appalled, but John ignored him and continued towards the orchestra. At the pit, the twin violin players already waited by the edge with extended arms. Other members waved, and the sight of everyone united together again offered a certain, steady comfort. A few moments of joviality transpired between John and the musicians. He mentioned that he eagerly anticipated their performance.

Patrick sat rigidly, his back a fine imitation of a wooden plank, and he remained mute when John sat beside him. Whenever attentions veered away from him, this species of reaction emerged. Fortunately this malady was fleeting and easily palliated.

"What is your assessment of this theater?" John asked, motioning broadly with his hand and looking towards the desolate balconies.

Patrick hesitated, vehemently attempting to sustain his posture and silence, but he simply did not possess the willpower to resist addressing an inquiry requesting his opinion. "Bad looking it's not," Patrick said, leaning forward. "It must have once been gorgeous. But one can see the disrepair," he said, jostling his loose seat. Patrick, in addition to his brilliance with languages, had a superb eye for colors and a far-reaching knowledge of interior design.

"I don't believe inordinate funds would be required to refurbish this place," John said.

"No," Patrick said, surveying the surroundings. "They would not. Hopefully it's mostly surface damage."

The show was about to begin. The normally lean audience was even sparer than usual, as no more than twenty-five people were present. With the dimming lights, John gradually exhaled.

❦

"Not too bad," Patrick said, clapping as the curtain closed for intermission.

"I'm off to the lobby," John said, with full confidence he would not be alone.

"Shall we?"

The white marble lobby attracted the entire audience. The fact that the attendance was so meager fused those who had shown into an unspoken comradeship, with everybody acknowledging each other with nod or smile. John was sure to lead Patrick to the center of the lobby. An older gentleman with a sienna bowtie began speaking to them with resolution about the stage and scenery and its suspect color schemes. Patrick was amenable, evidently approving of this company, for his habitual alternative reaction was icy silence.

While they conversed, John was startled to spot a familiar figure slip into the far corner of the lobby. She stared unwaveringly at him. Lavinia it was, and she remained deep in the corner, not desiring to attract the attention of the others. He was surprised she had left the backstage; usually, if she wanted John's company, a hand-delivered message would materialize beside him. Her staring persisted. She wanted to speak, although he surmised the topic would not be trifling fare due to her solemn expression. The moment was certainly not right to meet, but quickly addressing her would at least remove her from her vulnerable situation.

John extricated himself from his company by gently wandering away, aware that any precipitate movement would arouse Patrick's interest. As he crossed the lobby, he exchanged nods with those in his path. Lavinia shrank back through a door into the orchestra and into the private side hallway. The tiny corridor was inhabited solely by stretched shadows.

"I saw you in the audience," she declared. Meager lighting and heavy eyeliner imparted her with a spectral appearance.

"That much I deduced."

"I haven't seen you for a while."

John did not wish to review his travels. "It's good to see you."

Lavinia looked away, the back of her hand against her forehead. Her lengthy hair was elaborately braided. "I have to admit I am angry."

"You don't have to admit anything."

"I am," she said. "Angry at you."

"May I be so presumptuous as to ask why?"

Her hand fell to her side. "You chose not to come anymore."

"What?"

"To the opera," she said, while gripping the green fabric of her dress. "You made your decision."

John shook his head, prompting Lavinia's lips to purse. "I have simply missed a few weeks," John stated. "I don't know if that qualifies, when referring to opera attendance, as 'not coming anymore'."

Lavinia was not amused. Her response was to gnash her teeth and simmer. That she was annoyed was not especially surprising, yet it was the depth of her angst that mystified him. He attempted, for the moment, to eschew further discussion of it.

"The show is pleasing the audience tonight."

Lavinia didn't even glance at him.

"I must go now," John said. "As I'm sure you know, I'm here with a friend." He turned away.

"I know that you saw me there," she said.

When John turned back, a transfigured being stood before him. Her shoulders arched forward, she constricted her bloodless fingertips, and she gazed ruefully into an abyss of darkness above. The anger had siphoned away and she had succumbed to distress. It dawned on John: she was referring to the day by the train station when he had witnessed her laboring in the grimy kitchen of the placintarie shop, when he witnessed her being debased by a customer. He had hoped she hadn't noticed his presence. But the ghastliness of her current logic now became evident: he, unbeknownst to her, had departed for Turda the next day, and she assuredly believed that his sighting of her in that decrepit environment prompted his shunning of the theater. No wonder her bitterness.

"Working by the train station," she said. "I know you saw me."

"Yes," John said, aloofly. "I recall, a few weeks ago I believe. And?"

She hesitated, unsure of how to construe his blitheness. "And you never returned after that."

The shadows shifted. "Well first of all, the fact that we are engaged in conversation at the theater during an intermission disproves the 'never'," John said. She didn't react. "Also, it would have been quite difficult for me to attend these last weeks, considering I have been away from Cluj, although I suppose methods such as hiring a private helicopter to escort me to shows might have worked."

Lavinia's pointed shoes stroked the red carpet. "You saw me in those rags, dripping with oil in that horrific place. You heard that man whistling at me."

"That apron was rather becoming," John said.

"It must have bothered you."

"That it did."

"I knew it," she declared.

"Because I must say, and no offense, I heard you really don't make very good placintas; more salt is needed."

She perceptibly smiled, but waited for him to say more. She needed more.

"Look, I can care less where you work," John said. He moved closer to her. "At the same time, I understand your feelings. One would think with the level you have reached with your career on the stage, employed by the theater fulltime, that could sustain you."

"I'm sorry to complain to you, John. Maybe it's absurd. But when I'm working in that place, they humiliate me all day," she said, contending to remain composed. "I don't ask for so much and I certainly live simply. But often I, like the others, miss rehearsals because of our situations."

John heard shuffling outside. "It's time you get backstage."

"Yes, of course," she said, straightening.

"I'll be watching. And enjoying."

"Thank you for still coming," she said as she hurried down the hallway, her bulbous dress rustling loudly and passing into dimness.

In the lobby, only Patrick and his bowtied friend remained. Patrick signaled John with a histrionic wave, although the necessity of this gesture was dubitable since John was now four feet away.

"Shall we go back?" John said.

"I would like to think so," Patrick said, dryly. They shook hands with the older gentleman, who gracefully climbed the wide stairs towards the mezzanine. It was then that John noticed Tibi. He was towering above the stairs, glaring down at them from the carved railing. He turned violently away when John spotted him, but John was contented, for the moment, that he had been successful.

"Did you amuse yourself?" Patrick said.

"Pardon?"

"Amuse yourself off on your escapades."

Patrick's embellishment of situations, regardless of his knowledge of the scenario, could always be relied on. And there is a comfort in reliability, no matter how outrageous. For all Patrick knew, John could have been visiting the lavatory. Although, John admitted to himself, his description this time wasn't entirely fallacious. A bit of goading was called for. "Yes, I did," John said. "Although I cannot determine if my delight was due to the escapade itself, or the dearth of your presence on it."

The following half of the show was well performed, and the applause, albeit emanating from rationed sources, was at least hearty. John, of course, stood for the curtain call.

They made their way towards the lobby. Once again, John was certain to position Patrick in the room's center and converse. After a minute, it was time to look at the staircase above. While this might sound a simple task, it assuredly was not; it was a gruesome one. John steadied himself and then glanced atop the stairs. Tibi glowered down at him, his disturbing form heaving. Patrick never noticed, and John smoothly led him to the exit.

"A pleasant outing it was," John said. "And, might it be noted, it was so even without libations or melees. What on earth hath becometh of us?"

"Well said," Patrick said, lightly clapping and laughing. "And a stimulating question to ponder as well."

"I'll see you soon."

Patrick was confused. "Aren't you leaving?"

"Yes," John said, "but not at the moment. I will see you soon, OK?"

Providentially, Patrick offered no resistance. He likely had elsewhere he planned on going, presumably to meet his friend.

John remained. His back was to the stairs, and he stared out through the entrance doors into the night. A mist had settled. The avenue and the Piata Avram Iancu were still. The audience had faded away. He took a few steps outside; chilly, damp air greeted him and the wet cobblestone drive emitted a salient, granite odor. The clouds to the north were lustrous due to the partially concealed moon. It was only a matter of time, and he worked to calm himself and breathe steadily. It was only a matter of time.

"Enjoy the show?"

Tibi's bass voice was instantly recognizable and seemed inches away. For all his size, he moved soundlessly.

"Your cigar is a pleasure this evening?" John inquired. He had yet to see or smell the cigar, but was confident of its presence. Tibi's deep, paced laughter confirmed his assumption.

"You had company tonight," Tibi said.

John turned. The glow of Tibi's cigar contrasted with the

darkness, and his tuxedo was stretched with his massive presence. The glowing fluctuated. Tibi certainly would not directly inquire, but he was rabid to know how John knew Patrick, and more crucially, how much, if anything, Patrick had informed him about Tibi's curious jaunts to France. "I did. I had this perplexing premonition that there might be a few empty seats and wanted to help."

Tibi failed to respond and had yet to move.

The miasma of smoke had arrived and now enveloped John. "And alas, I was right. Empty seats."

Tibi pulled on his cigar.

"So much I'm hearing lately," John said. He stepped to his left, and looked up through the dimness at the theater's lengthy Doric columns.

"Oh?"

"Information, you know how it interminably travels. Even when one is not seeking it, it arrives."

"So thus you have heard positive reviews of my show?" Tibi asked. His thin eyes were barely visible.

"Hearing those reviews requires advertisement, which we both know doesn't exist for this theater," John said, dryly.

Tibi exhaled a tentacle of bluish smoke.

John was hesitant, this was certain, but he needed to forge forward, and directly so. "I did have the good fortune of hearing about some news though."

"Did you."

"Yes, absolutely. A new investment company forming. And lo and behold, with you as one of the owners."

He did not respond.

"It will be quite large, with international investments, from what I heard."

Tibi lowered his cigar. "What is your interest in this matter?"

"None," John said, "Except I also heard need a head financial analyst."

Tibi's steady laughter sounded submerged. "That might be true, but we are hiring Romanians, not Americans," he said, continuing to laugh.

"Excellent," John said. "Fortunately I know the right person."

"Oh?" Tibi said, surprised. "Who might that be?" he asked, shifting to a mocking tone.

"A person who graduated atop the business and economics programs at the University, and has helped greatly with the success of other companies."

"I see."

"She would be perfect."

"*She?*" Tibi said, laughing. "This 'she' might not be appropriate. You think me a bit too modern." He returned his cigar to his sallow lips. "And I believe I've entertained your intrusions into affairs that don't concern you for long enough."

John looked back towards the avenue. The mist had settled to street level, forming a dense, silvery shroud that was stealthily advancing upon them. "I don't normally intrude."

"Then you're not as foolish as I was beginning to suspect," Tibi said, coldly.

John envisioned Alina in Turda, encircled by bickering customers at the market. "For example, I haven't intruded upon your travel itineraries," John said, continuing to peruse the mist, but ensuring Tibi remained peripherally visible.

Tibi seemed to continuously swell.

"Or I haven't intruded upon the nature of your trips. For example, to France," John said. Tibi's form ossified; his breathing halted. "Now of course there is much to see in France, I certainly acknowledge that." John had to press on. "But I don't even intrude upon the bank deposits you make there."

Silence predominated, shattered only by the reconstructed car engine striving to accelerate past the theater. John, realizing his teeth were incising into his lower lip, released their grip, tasting the copper of blood.

"You have gone a step too far," Tibi said.

"Perhaps."

"It would be wise to abandon your nonchalant attitude."

John was far from nonchalant.

"I have much influence here," Tibi said. "You are not in the safety of your home country."

"I'm from New York; it can get rather dangerous back there too."

"You cannot always sit drinking your bottles of wine in your top floor Iuliu Maniu apartment," Tibi said, as John turned to him.

So he had researched him.

"Surprised?" Tibi said, moving forward. "Let us be serious, John. You're not safe here. Tonight you could vanish, tonight you could disappear, and not one person would know. So don't be more foolish than you already are."

Tibi's connections in numerous industries were pervasive, and he was already fully prepared to carry his threats through. John's temptation to abandon this course, and return to his solitude and his wine was intoxicating. The velvet mist now swaddled their feet. Adamancy was vital.

"Nobody cares about you John, or what happens to you," Tibi said, staring malevolently. "Look at how you sit alone at all these shows. You're a pathetic figure."

"In fairness, I did have someone with me this evening."

He moved closer, dreadfully close, dropping his cigar onto the misty cobblestones and mashing it with his polished shoe. "Don't be surprised at what I know about you, John Arden. And know well that I can have you crushed." John felt Tibi's rancid breath moist

229

and thick on his neck. His baleful eyes were blood red.

He realized that Tibi must have considered him a threat from the moment he had first seen him months ago. But this was John's time. "I'm not asking you for favors," John said. "I'm actually trying to do you one."

"And how do you come to such a conclusion?"

"The person I'm recommending is the finest. It's that simple. As I said, she was number one in her university, and is brilliant in the workplace; these aren't debatable conclusions. She can make the difference. And if you know so much about me, as you state, then you should be aware that I know what I'm talking about." John's shoulders were squared with Tibi's. "In these times where business success is so elusive, so rare, what I'm recommending to you is a way for the new company to be a resounding triumph."

Tibi stared at John. "What is your interest in all this?"

"To ensure the right thing happens."

Tibi's form now oscillated. As the clouds pulled away, his coarse beard appeared reddish in the moonlight. "I'm not the sole owner," Tibi said. "There is a group of owners who also have a say in the hiring. And I'm not involved in the day-to-day company affairs at all. It is merely an investment."

"I'm confident your 'influence', which you have recently lauded and referred to in conjunction with my fragile existence, will have no problem getting anything done," John said. "Including giving significant pay raises to this opera cast and orchestra that toil so relentlessly to produce the lovely performances that we then reapeth."

"This is ridiculous," Tibi said, spitting out his words as his sizeable head turned sharply to the side.

"Not in the least."

"You are going too far."

"I'm not. I just detest scandals, and I don't want devastating information about you, Tibi, or perhaps *'Claude'* if you will," he said as Tibi's jaw palpitated, "in the hands of the authorities and embassies and all over the news. And then the investigations into all your financial affairs. A terrible mess it will be: ignominy, lost money, jail — it would be awful." John shuddered dramatically. "I just don't want all that. Neither do you. But we can both avoid that very simply," John said. "And those pay raises, which I expect to hear about immediately and which I will check on, will allow your loyal, paying audience to be treated to a happier cast and better shows." John watched him probe his beard. "Do you wish to deny us that?"

Tibi grunted.

"Now in reference to my safety, I am not so confident or nonchalant about it as you suggest. I must shamefully confess that. Perhaps that is why I placed all this terrible information about you in the hands of another," John said, bluffing. "And if anything happens to me, anything, be sure it will be immediately disseminated to all the proper places."

Tibi's nostrils flared.

"But let us forget about these horrendous things, and return to my generous recommendation on how to guarantee the new investment company's triumphant success," John said.

"How do I know you won't want even more after this?" Tibi said.

John rubbed his hands together. "Notice I'm not asking for anything for myself," John said. "Take care of my requests, and you'll hear no more from me."

Tibi's black leather shoe scraped the ground. The sodden remnants of his cigar lay strewn across cobblestones, buried beneath mist. "So what is her name?"

# Chapter 21

The canopy of green filtered the sunlight. John reclined on a bench, stretching his legs onto the gravel path. Through his sandals he felt warmth emanating from the heated stones.

It was midday Sunday, and many spirited people strolled along the path in the Parcul Central. It was the first day short sleeve shirts and even short pants were commonplace. The young lawns were chartreuse, and the robins chirped from above. Nearby John, a boy and girl were intent upon catching a third child, a swift girl, who was successfully eluding them to the delight of all.

He was appreciating his last days in Cluj. On Thursday afternoon he was departing: a flight back to New York. He had been away a very long time. Flashes appeared of the avenues of Manhattan, of the towering grey buildings, of the surging crowds. Certainly, he experienced trepidation about returning, but for the first time he felt prepared to return, to finally face the ashes of his former vapid existence. Now he was hopeful, at long last, that he could create something meaningful.

It had been three weeks since he confronted Tibi at the Opera.

He had heard that Alina interviewed for head financial analyst at the new company, and she had received the position the next day. She must have already begun working. John shifted on the bench to allow sunrays to bathe his face. With eyes closed everything intensified: the fluttering of the robins' wings and the laughter, as well as the warmth of the sun.

Time passed undetected, his senses alert, and eventually he heard the steady crunching of gravel cease directly before him. It did not resume. He opened his eyes, and it was difficult to see who stood before him due to the blinding light. But that magnificent form; yes, he believed it was Alina. The sun, positioned directly behind her, blurred her image into the celestial.

"Were you involved with my job?" the form inquired.

It was she.

"Is that another of your fashionable ways of saying 'hello'?"

"Were you?"

"Your question is unclear." John said.

She hadn't moved. "Did you help get me that job?"

John shifted on the bench to observe her from an angle. Her long hair draped loosely, and her immense eyes were fixated upon him. "Bogdan is the only person I know working for your Turda store, and I met him after you began, so I couldn't have been much help."

She paused. "My new job."

"Almost any response besides 'what new job?' shall implicate me," John said. That she had discovered his involvement was no surprise, considering the propensity for information to seep out, regardless of confidentiality.

She sat beside him on the bench, no longer looking at him. Exhaling slowly, she gently massaged her forehead. "I am a bit perturbed about you helping to arrange things," she said. "Part of me is upset."

A tall man carrying a tennis racket passed them. He practiced his backhand, swatting phantom balls in the warm air. His imaginary match must have been progressing favorably, for his swinging was accompanied by a mirthful comportment.

"Upset?"

"Your helping me get that position," she said. "It's something I wanted to earn."

John laughed, naturally and freely. "If one thing is clear enough, it is that you did earn it," he said, turning towards her. "Otherwise, and please don't be offended by this or bludgeon me with a blunt object, but I would not have helped you in that way."

"You believe I earned that job?" Alina said. She knew her abilities, yet the sole person whose assurance mattered to her was John's, and she was no longer hesitant to seek it.

"Shall we be honest?" John said.

"Of course."

"You know you're the most qualified for that job; you know no one can help the company and help its employees more than you." She nodded, but a touch of pride was still in the way. John raised a handful of gravel from the path and cherished the contrast between the heated top stones and chilly, damp ones beneath. "But in these times, ascertaining that opportunity is nearly impossible, and it is not based on merit," he said. "Now that opportunity is finally yours, and I sense you will create smoother paths for others."

Alina placed her hands on her lap. Her body relaxed. "It is true," she said, exuberantly. "The position has been superb. Challenging, formidable in the ways I had always been seeking." She leaned forward. "And I know you would be impressed by the way I'm now interacting with my work colleagues and associates. Although in truth John, you might miss the old thrashings I used to deal them," she said laughing. Her eyes flashed. "Thank you so much for that."

Seeing her vitalized was a wonder. It was the first time he witnessed that unmitigated luminance permeating her expression. A breeze shifted the branches, prompting their slender shadows to slide across her exquisite face. She moved closer to John.

"What will you be doing these days?" she asked.

The wild chestnut leaves rustled. "I'm returning to New York."

Alina's back straightened. "When?"

"Thursday."

"For how long," Alina said. "When are you coming back?"

A few bright yellow dandelion flowers poked undauntedly through sprouting lawns.

"Why are you going?" Alina said, still positioned stiffly upright.

"It's not about leaving here," John said. "It's about returning there."

Alina seized John's hand. "I've been wanting to talk to you ever since you left Turda," she said. "Embarrassing it is to admit, but I was utterly terrified about calling you."

John gently squeezed her hand.

"Terrified about the way I felt," Alina said. "But I'm not terrified anymore."

She was beside him. Hands interlocked. They kissed and felt warm throughout. They closed their eyes together and disappeared into this warmth.

She sat on the edge of his bed, and he traced the refined lines of her figure. It was early Thursday morning, and she needed to depart for work. Her day was replete with meetings and conferences. His flight left at one that afternoon. Except for the suitcases by the door, his apartment was bare; the desolate rooms began to fill with pale morning light. They had savored the last nights together. The future had not been mentioned, but they had relished the present.

"I do hope that one day you will return," she said.

John felt the softness of her back with his fingertips, and admired her lengthy hair. "You are magnificent," he said.

They hugged for the longest time at the door. Neither wanted to release his or her grip. They kissed. Atop the staircase, in the silent hallway, they held hands and kissed once again. Alina finally turned away sharply, descending the worn flights of limestone stairs. He heard the building door shut and dashed into his apartment. From his front windows he watched her striding down Iuliu Maniu. She was the only soul on the street. Her steps were long, confident, and he was proud. Observing her, he experienced fathomless tremors of optimism for all he had encountered on his journeys here. Her hand dabbed her cheeks. The road became thinner and her elegant figure became smaller and more difficult to see. He leaned out the window, grasping its base. The early morning air was still callow and cool. She hesitated at the street corner, he leaned farther, and then she turned down the side road and out of his view.

A half an hour later he strolled for a final time by the Somes River. It flowed swiftly and with conviction and John could hear the water slipping over smooth stones in the shallow parts. The reliable fishermen were present in grand numbers; they were enjoying the warm spring day. They reclined on the sloped riverbanks with their fishing poles extended over the rushing water.

As John passed the Parcul de Sport, alongside where the river widened, he halted at the sight of a particular person. He hoped, dearly. Yes, it was: his old friend the beneficent fisherman. It had been months since he had shared his palinca with a lonely and disconsolate John.

John sat beside him, and the fisherman turned. As he recognized John, the corners of his eyes crinkled, his eyes moistened, and he rested a hand on John's shoulder. His face was tanned and leathery, and he extended his arm, offering his sunflower seeds from a clear bag. John accepted them, knowing he would struggle to remove seed from shell, and that he would amuse the fisherman with his antic attempts. As they lay back and surveyed the river, the fresh smell of earth and grass was brisk. The day was warming and the sun shown brilliantly.

After some time, the fisherman jumped up and struggled with the fishing pole. John was startled. The fisherman pulled at the line. Some thrashing, and silver emerged from the water; it was a thin fish. He reeled it in and cradled the body as it flapped in his hands. Droplets of cold water splashed onto John's face. He wondered where the fisherman would store this fish for he had no containers. The fisherman stepped to the river's edge, and kneeled. He lowered his hands inches from the water and released the fish, which quickly swam away. The sunlight dappled the river's surface.

Breinigsville, PA USA
01 April 2011
258941BV00002B/1/P